The Baby-sitter Burglaries

Nancy heard banging. It was coming from a Dumpster next to the building. Then she heard a child sobbing. Nancy half-skated, half-ran to the Dumpster and threw open the lid. Carlos was inside. He looked up at her, tears streaking his face.

"Oh, Carlos," Nancy said. "How did you—never mind. Can you grab my hand?" She leaned down, reaching for him, but wasn't close enough. She leaned in farther until she was on tiptoe, balancing on the edge of the Dumpster, stretching as far as she could. "Carlos—take my hand!"

Carlos's fingers touched Nancy's hand. Then she froze in horror. Someone had grabbed her legs and flipped her body up and over the edge of the Dumpster. Nancy fell hard into the bottom of the Dumpster. The lid slammed shut, leaving her in the dark, facedown in garbage!

Nancy Drew
Mystery Stories

Available from Simon & Schuster

NANCY DREW® 129

THE BABY-SITTER BURGLARIES

CAROLYN KEENE

Aladdin Paperbacks
New York   London   Toronto   Sydney   Singapore

First Aladdin Paperbacks edition January 2002
First Minstrel edition February 1996

Copyright © 1996 by Simon & Schuster, Inc.
Produced by Mega-Books, Inc.

ALADDIN PAPERBACKS
An imprint of Simon & Schuster
Children's Publishing Division
1230 Avenue of the Americas
New York, NY 10020

Printed in U.S.A.
10 9 8 7 6

NANCY DREW and THE NANCY DREW MYSTERY STORIES are registered trademarks of Simon & Schuster, Inc.
ISBN 0-671-50507-6

Contents

THE BABY-SITTER
BURGLARIES

1

Baby-sitter or Burglar?

"How did he do that?" George Fayne asked. She leaned forward on the edge of the sofa and stared at the television set. "Nancy Drew, put that book down and look at this."

They were sitting on the sofa in Nancy's living room. Nancy looked at the screen.

A magician was waving his arms over a woman, who was lying on a table. The sequins on her costume sparkled like thousands of tiny gold coins. The magician lifted his hand, and the woman's body rose slowly, then floated a few feet over the table. The magician drew a hoop up and down her body. No invisible wires were holding her up.

"Can you believe that?" George asked Nancy. "It looks so real." She brushed her short, dark curls away from her eyes.

Nancy shook her head. "I've heard that magicians can levitate people, but it has to be a trick—it looks impossible," she said. Her blue eyes flashed, and she grinned. "Bet I can make that magician disappear—just like that."

She picked up the remote control and pointed it at the television set. She clicked, and the screen went dark. "See? Like magic," she said, laughing.

George groaned and threw a pillow at her. "Please, Nancy—find a new mystery to solve," she said. "Don't torture your friends with bad magic tricks."

Nancy picked up the pillow and aimed it at George. The phone on the table beside her rang. She dropped the pillow and picked up the receiver. "Ouch!" she cried out, and held it away from her ear. Voices were screaming at her. Then a calm voice broke into the noise. "Boys, please get off the phone—it's my turn to talk now."

Nancy brushed her reddish blond hair behind her ear. "Bess? Is that you?" she asked. Bess Marvin was George's cousin, and Nancy felt as if she'd been friends with both of them forever.

"Nancy? I'm so glad you're home," Bess said. Nancy heard shouts and loud laughter in the background. It was hard to understand what Bess was saying.

Nancy heard a loud click in her ear. "Wait! Bess?" She looked over at George, who looked back at Nancy with raised eyebrows.

"What's going on?" George asked.

"I don't know," Nancy said. "Bess said something about baby-sitting. We're supposed to meet her at Twenty-four Sycamore Lane. I think our sunny spring morning is about to get more lively."

Sycamore Lane in River Heights was guarded by rows of ancient sycamore trees, their branches dotted with buds. Nancy pulled her blue Mustang in front of a two-story house with the name Puentes painted on the mailbox.

They got out of the car and walked up the front steps onto the porch. The door flew open, jerking the knob out of Nancy's hand. Bess stood in the doorway, holding a wailing little dark-haired girl. Bess's metallic blue sweater and leggings were speckled with oatmeal, but she was smiling as she greeted Nancy. Then she laughed at George. "Come on in, George. The kids won't bite. I promise."

Nancy and George stepped into the living room, then ducked as a soccer ball flew past their heads. Nancy straightened up slowly, looking around for other flying missiles.

"Over here, boys," Bess said firmly, crooking her finger at the four boys galloping around the Puentes living room. They ran up to Bess.

"We don't throw things in the house," she told them. "Now, I'd like you to meet Nancy and

3

George." Bess patted the heads of two small blond boys. "These brothers are Michael and Mitchell, and their friends are Kyle and Brian." The boys shouted a greeting, then dashed off to play.

Bess sat down in a rocking chair and picked up the little girl, whose wail had become a sniffle. "And this is Sara," Bess said. "Blow." She wiped Sara's nose. "Sara's a little upset because the boys want to build a fort with sheets and they won't let her help. They think she's too little." Sara's lower lip quivered, and she hid her face in Bess's long blond hair.

Nancy leaned forward and smiled. "Oh, poor Sara. Maybe we can change their minds."

Sara looked hopeful, then flung her arms out to Nancy. Nancy gathered her up in a hug, but when she tried to put Sara back on Bess's lap, the little girl's hand stuck to Nancy's hair.

Bess chuckled as she gently separated Sara's hand from Nancy's hair. "I hate to tell you this, Nancy, but . . ."

"Oh, no," Nancy said. She pulled a sticky strand of hair away from her cheek, wishing she had seen the lollipop in Sara's hand.

A boy jumped out from behind the sofa, shouting, "Carlos to the rescue!" He had curly dark hair and brown eyes flashing with mischief. He caught sight of George and flung himself at her knees, ramming his head into her stomach.

"Ooof! Easy, Carlos," Bess said. "Uh, Nancy, this is Carlos Puentes."

George smiled weakly down at him. "He's on the Pee Wee soccer team I coach."

"He's also Juanita's little brother," Bess said. "Carlos is home on spring vacation from second grade. He lives here with Juanita and their grandfather, Diego Puentes, the magician."

"I'm glad to meet you, Carlos," Nancy said. *Six* children, she thought. Bess is baby-sitting *six* children.

Nancy moved a pile of sheets and sat on the sofa opposite Bess. "Is this your new job?" she asked.

"No—it's Juanita's weekly play group," Bess explained. "You remember Juanita. She graduated two years ahead of us at River Heights High. She and Carlos have been living with their grandfather since their parents died. I asked her if I could help her today—these kids are so adorable." Bess bounced Sara on her knee, making her giggle.

"You *asked* for this?" Nancy said, shaking her head.

"So where's Juanita?" George hobbled over to join them, with Carlos still attached to her leg.

"She's at the police station," Bess replied. "Juanita baby-sits for some families in River Estates. They've had a few burglaries there lately. The police want to find out whether

Juanita saw or heard anything while she was baby-sitting."

Nancy nodded. "I remember reading about the burglaries in the paper."

Nancy looked down at Carlos. He was sitting on the floor tying George's shoelaces together. Bess gave him a stern look. Carlos grinned and ran off to join the other boys. George looked down at her shoes in surprise and bent down to fix the laces. Nancy laughed.

"Anyway," Bess continued. "Juanita never expected to leave anyone else in charge of the play group, but the police wanted to speak to her right away. I told her I'd call you guys, so the kids would have plenty of supervision."

"Thanks a lot," George said.

Bess stood up, still holding Sara. "Could you play with the boys while I clean up Sara a little?" Bess asked. When George nodded, Bess headed for the kitchen.

Nancy looked for the boys. "Uh-oh. Where did they go?" she asked George.

Carlos and the other boys raced into the living room. Each was holding an open cereal box. As if on cue, they dug their hands into the boxes and flung cereal into the air. George and Nancy gasped while the boys ran in circles around them yelling, "Look—it's snowing!"

"Wait—boys—please," Nancy begged. "George, you coach Pee Wee—can't you do something?"

"Like what?" George asked, frantically scooping up cereal from the rug. "Kids don't act this way at soccer practice—their parents are with them."

Nancy looked around in desperation. The living room was beginning to look like a cereal bowl. She had to stop them before they ran and got the milk.

The boys gave Nancy challenging stares while she sized up the situation. She grabbed a sheet off the couch and draped it over two armchairs. She crawled under the sheet. The boys knelt down to peek under the sheet.

"Come on in," Nancy said. "But put down the cereal boxes first." The boys giggled, threw the boxes down, and piled in. "Isn't this a great fort?" Nancy asked, "We could build it bigger in the backyard, hang sheets over a rope tied between the trees. Want to try it?"

The boys yelled and cheered. Over their noise, Nancy heard a loud knocking on the front door. She peeked out from under the sheet.

Bess hurried into the room. She opened the door cautiously, then stepped back with a gasp. A snarling Doberman pinscher stood in the doorway, barely restrained on a leash held by a tall woman, who was frowning.

"I am Alice Mendenhall," she said. "And I want to talk to Juanita!"

Nancy scrambled up, pulling the sheets off her

7

head. "I'm sorry, Ms. Mendenhall, but Juanita's not—"

"Don't tell me she's not here—I want to talk to her *now!* And it's *Mrs.* Mendenhall."

Mrs. Mendenhall had graying brown hair and wore what looked like pajamas. She waved a plastic dump truck in Nancy's face. "Those kids are throwing toys over my fence! Do you know what this is?" she asked Nancy. "It's plastic. Buster could die if he eats plastic. Are you trying to kill my dog?"

Nancy held out her hand for the truck and said calmly, "Look, I'm sorry that someone threw toys over the fence, but we're just filling in for Juanita. I'm sure when she gets back she'll—"

Straining at his leash and barking, Buster snapped at the truck in Nancy's hand. The children ran out of the room, screaming. George ran after them.

Mrs. Mendenhall jerked Buster back to her side. "I work the night shift at the bakery, and I have to sleep during the day. If Juanita can't keep those kids quiet and away from my fence—I'll find a way," she said. Mrs. Mendenhall left, dragging Buster down the steps.

Nancy started picking up the cereal. "Buster sure knows how to empty a room, doesn't he?"

"What happened, Nancy?" Bess asked. "This room is a disaster!"

8

"Sorry, Bess, it's been a long time since I baby-sat," Nancy said. "I should have tried to distract the boys in the first place. Don't worry, we'll get it cleaned up. Will you hand me that wastebasket?" Nancy scooped up cereal with her hands and tossed it into the wastebasket. "Juanita sure has her hands full, doesn't she?"

Bess started gathering up the sheets. "Yes, but she's wonderfully patient with the kids," she said. "She even wants to run a nursery school someday. She's taking classes at the university to get a degree in child psychology."

Bess folded a sheet and shook her head. "I don't know when Juanita has time to study," she said. "She runs this play group every Friday. Then she baby-sits in the evenings and sets up birthday parties for her grandfather."

George poked her head in. "I'm going to take the kids outside and get started on that fort, okay?"

"Yes—please!" Nancy said as Bess handed George the sheets.

Nancy was vacuuming a few minutes later when she heard the front door open. A young woman with long, curly black hair and dark brown eyes came into the living room.

"Hi, Juanita," said Nancy, turning off the vacuum. "Do you remember me? Nancy Drew?"

"Oh, Nancy. Of course I do. Bess said you might come over. I'm so glad to see you." Juanita

9

turned to Bess. "I'm sorry," she said, "I had no idea it would take so long downtown."

"That's okay," Bess said. "But you look terrible, Juanita. What's the matter?" she asked.

Juanita looked at Bess and Nancy with tears in her eyes. "The police almost arrested me," she said. "They think I'm a burglar."

2

Not So Secure

Bess stared at Juanita. "You? A burglar? I don't believe it!"

Juanita sighed. "Thanks, Bess," she said, "but three of my regular customers in River Estates were robbed in the past two weeks."

"But why do they think you're the thief?" Nancy asked.

"Because I had evening baby-sitting jobs at those houses—and because of David," Juanita said. She knelt to pick up Sara's blocks.

Nancy touched Juanita's shoulder and said, "Who's David?"

Juanita's face turned pink. "David Andrews. He's my boyfriend. He used to work for the Secure Monitoring Company, and he's the one who installed the security systems in the houses that were robbed."

It did seem suspicious, Nancy thought, that

both a baby-sitter and her boyfriend had been in the burgled houses.

"Do the police think you and David worked together to break into the houses?" Nancy asked.

Juanita nodded, clasping her hands tightly together. Nancy glimpsed a face through the window behind Juanita. Was that Mrs. Mendenhall? Whoever it was, the window was now empty.

"Well, you can stop worrying right now, Juanita," Bess said loyally, patting Juanita's hand. "Nancy is a terrific detective. She'll prove you're innocent."

"I'll do my best," Nancy said.

Juanita relaxed. "Thanks, Nancy," she said. "Come on into the kitchen and we'll have lunch."

"We're right behind you," said Bess, leading the way.

The boys stomped in from the backyard. George followed, carrying Sara. Bess whispered to George, filling her in on Juanita's near arrest.

Juanita seated the children and found each one's lunch box. They eagerly opened them and began to unwrap their food while Juanita heated up some stew for Nancy and her friends.

At the same time, Juanita managed to listen to Sara's soft chatter, wipe up Michael's spilled juice, and catch Carlos's chair just before he tipped over. She seemed to have eyes in the back of her head.

"Hey, Nita! That dragon lady came over with her dog!" Carlos yelled.

Worry lines deepened on Juanita's forehead. "Mrs. Mendenhall was here?" She set out a loaf of bread and plates, and Bess helped her with the silverware.

"How did you know he was talking about Mrs. Mendenhall?" George asked.

Juanita smiled. "Because that's what Carlos always calls her," she said. She brought the stew to the table, and the girls passed it around and helped themselves. "It smells delicious," said Bess.

Nancy ate some stew and said, "This is fabulous!"

George broke off a piece of bread to mop up the gravy. "Mrs. Mendenhall said the kids had thrown plastic toys over the fence for her Doberman to eat."

"We *have* been missing a few toys. I'll try to watch the kids more closely," Juanita said. "But Mrs. Mendenhall is always complaining, mostly about the noise. I'm trying to get a day care license, so that the play group can be daily instead of just on Fridays. But I'm afraid I might see Mrs. Mendenhall and Buster daily, too—complaining."

After lunch was over, Juanita led the children to the living room for quiet time. Nancy, George, and Bess cleaned up the kitchen and joined her after they finished. Bess stopped to look at a pile of printed flyers on a table. "Juanita!" she exclaimed. "This is a great picture of Diego." She picked up a flyer and waved it. "Did you help him make these flyers?"

Juanita nodded. "Besides advertising his magic shows," she said, "they give the address and hours of the Magic Shop." Juanita handed flyers to Nancy and George.

Nancy looked at the photograph on the flyer. Diego the Great looked like the perfect magician. He wore a black top hat and cloak and had a long gray mustache.

"David's been working at the Magic Shop full time ever since he left Secure Monitoring Company," Juanita said. "Grandfather rented him the apartment on the second floor, above the store. Grandfather's so busy he had to hire another assistant to help during the magic shows."

"When did Diego hire him?" Bess asked, surprised.

"About two weeks ago," Juanita said. "Yes, that's right, because it was a Wednesday. March twelfth, I think. Max showed up with a letter from a magic supply dealer recommending him as an assistant. You'll like the new show, Bess— it's more fun with two assistants."

Nancy put the flyer in her purse, then pulled out a notebook. "Can you give me the names of all your baby-sitting customers in River Estates?" she asked Juanita.

Juanita looked worried again. "I hope you can

solve this mystery, Nancy," she said. "Someone's breaking into those houses, but it's not me and David." She recited the names and addresses of her customers, and Nancy wrote them down.

Carlos found a notebook and pencil. "I want to be a detective, too," he said. He chewed on his lip and scribbled as fast as he could.

At last, Nancy closed her notebook and looked up at Juanita. "We'll see you later, okay? I need to talk to the police about the burglaries. Try not to worry."

"I'll try," Juanita whispered. "But you know, Nancy, no one will hire me if people find out I'm a suspect in three burglaries."

Twenty minutes later, Nancy, Bess, and George were at the River Heights police station. A young police officer behind the front desk asked, "Can I help you?"

"Is Chief McGinnis in his office?" Nancy asked her. Chief McGinnis had been helpful with many of Nancy's cases in River Heights.

"The chief is on vacation, Ms. Drew," a familiar voice said. "Guess you'll have to talk to me." It was Officer Brody.

Nancy turned and looked warily at him. She'd dealt with him before, too, and he didn't always appreciate her questions. She followed him into his office while Bess and George waited in the lobby. He pointed out a chair to Nancy then sat behind his desk.

15

Nancy sat down and said, "I need some information on the recent burglaries in River Estates," she said.

"Let me guess," Officer Brody said sarcastically. "You just happen to be friends with Juanita Puentes and David Andrews, and you're trying to prove them innocent. Right?"

Nancy smiled. "Actually, I've never met David Andrews," she said. "But why do you think Juanita is involved?"

"River Estates has had three break-ins and burglaries in the last week and a half," Officer Brody said. "The Mowrer house was first on March eighteenth, then two days later the Bairds were hit, and the Larsens six days after that. And what do all three crimes have in common? Juanita Puentes and David Andrews. Puentes baby-sits at each house, and Andrews was the one who installed the security systems—that was before he was fired."

"Fired?" Nancy sat up straight.

"Fired," Officer Brody repeated. "Andrews installed the systems, and he knew the security codes for the houses. So either the owners never turned on the systems, or someone knew the security codes and turned off the alarms. No alarms sounded at any of the houses. And a Mrs. Alice Mendenhall, Juanita's neighbor, just called. She said she'd overheard Andrews talking about the Secure systems to some of the parents who dropped off their children at Juanita's play group. He might be setting up future burglaries."

So that was why Mrs. Mendenhall was slinking past Juanita's window. She was eavesdropping! She must have heard Juanita talking about the burglaries. But why had she told the police what she knew about David?

Officer Brody drummed his fingers on his desk. "I'm willing to bet that Puentes and her boyfriend are working together. She cases out the houses—finds out what they have. Then, when the owners are away—which she'd know—he comes back, disables the systems, and breaks into the houses," he said.

Nancy leaned forward. "But you don't have enough evidence to arrest them."

"Not yet," Officer Brody said. "Listen, I'll give you the addresses of the burgled houses. But don't get in my way." He gave her a steely look and handed her a paper.

Nancy took the paper. "Thank you," she said, "Don't worry. I won't get in your way." She stood up and tucked the paper into her purse. Officer Brody obviously hadn't changed his opinion about teenaged detectives.

Nancy left the police station with Bess and George, filling them in on her conversation with Officer Brody. George opened the door of Nancy's Mustang. "So what's next, Nancy?"

Nancy slid behind the wheel. "I think we

17

should talk to the owners of the burgled houses—the Mowrers, the Bairds, and the Larsens. Officer Brody gave me their addresses." She compared his list with the names and addresses Juanita had given her. The Mowrers, Bairds, and Larsens were all customers of Juanita.

They drove to River Estates, an affluent neighborhood only a few blocks from Juanita's house. Two-story houses stood on large lawns planted with fruit trees, oaks, and willows. Nancy stopped at the Baird house first and then at the Mowrer house, but neither family was home.

Nancy pulled the Mustang into the concrete driveway alongside the Larsen house. The three girls climbed out of the car.

Mrs. Larsen answered the doorbell. "Hello— can I help you?" she asked. Her daughter stood behind her, clinging to Mrs. Larsen's sleeve.

"I'm Nancy Drew, and these are my friends Bess Marvin and George Fayne," Nancy said. "I'm investigating the burglaries in the neighborhood. Do you have a minute to answer some questions?"

Mrs. Larsen hesitated, studying Nancy's face. "Nancy Drew? Oh yes—I remember you— you're that young detective. Your father is my lawyer. Please, come in," she said. "I was just going to put Melissa in for her nap. I'll be right back. Please go into the living room and make yourselves comfortable."

The living room had two flowered sofas facing each other and Oriental rugs artfully scattered on the floor. "What a beautiful room," Bess said.

When Mrs. Larsen returned to them, Nancy asked her about the security system. Mrs. Larsen showed her how all the windows and doors on the ground floor were wired. "If anyone tries to open them, it'll set off the alarm," she said.

Then she led them to a hallway near the garage. "This is the main control panel for the system," she said. The panel had rows of buttons, and a red light that glowed when the security system was turned on. "Nothing was disturbed on the panel when we arrived home and discovered the burglary," Mrs. Larsen said.

"How could that be?" George asked.

"The burglars broke in through an upstairs window. Come, I'll show you."

Mrs. Larsen led the girls upstairs and pointed out a window on the landing. The wood frame was split. "This is how they got in," she said. "They must have pried it open with a crowbar or something like that."

"But why didn't the alarm go off?" asked Nancy.

"The upstairs windows aren't wired to the security system." Mrs. Larsen pointed to the ceiling over the stairway. "That's a motion detector. It should have sent a signal to the alarm as soon as the burglars walked down the stairs. But it didn't. It's all very puzzling," she said.

"What happens when the alarm is set off?" Nancy asked.

"The signal goes to Secure Monitoring Company, and they contact the police immediately."

Nancy looked around the upstairs hall. "There's another control panel," she said. "It looks just like the one downstairs. Does it activate the system, too?" she asked.

Mrs. Larsen nodded. "I can turn the system on or off by punching in the security code on this panel or on the one downstairs."

"Did you have it on that day?" Bess asked.

Mrs. Larsen gave Bess an indignant look. "That's what Secure Monitoring asked me when they came over to check the system after the burglary. I *never* forget to set the alarm. The rest of the system is in the basement," she said. "Let's go downstairs."

Back on the ground floor, Nancy spoke to George. "Take a look around outside while we're in the basement. Since the Larsen burglary took place only two days ago, maybe you can find some footprints or other clues."

"Cool," George said, and she left the house.

Nancy and Bess followed Mrs. Larsen to the basement. She pointed out the wired metal bars on the basement windows. "And look here," she said. "These wires go up from the windows to the ceiling. They end up at that transmitter high on the wall over there."

Nancy hadn't seen that many security systems

to be an expert, but nothing looked damaged—the wires looked intact.

"Let's go see if George has found anything," Nancy said. They went out into the backyard. "No clues here, Nancy," said George. "Just a few dog tracks in the flower bed."

Mrs. Larsen stared at the tracks. "That's odd," she said. "We don't own a dog. And no pets are allowed to run loose in River Estates."

"And the yard is fenced," said Bess.

"What did the thieves take?" Nancy asked Mrs. Larsen.

"All they took was the TV set and the VCR. A few things are missing from the backyard, too," Mrs. Larsen said, "but they're not important."

"Did anyone outside your family know the security code?" Nancy asked.

Mrs. Larsen hesitated. "Well, normally I wouldn't give it out to anyone, but I did give the code to my neighbor, Reese Gardner. He offered to feed my cat while I was on vacation," she said.

Mrs. Larsen paused, wrinkling her forehead. "Oh, and I gave it to my baby-sitter—Juanita Puentes."

3

Snatched

Nancy's heart sank. Since Juanita knew the Larsens' security code, the police would definitely suspect her. "Why did you give Juanita your security code?" Nancy asked Mrs. Larsen.

Mrs. Larsen looked uncomfortable, then sighed. "I know it sounds like too many people knew the code. But Melissa accidentally pushed some buttons on the control panel while Juanita was baby-sitting. The alarm went off, so Juanita called me and I gave her the code over the phone so she could turn it off," she explained.

"Do the police know about this?" George asked.

Mrs. Larsen nodded. "They wanted to know whether Juanita baby-sat for anyone else in the neighborhood. Juanita is so good with children—nearly everyone I know hires her to baby-sit," Mrs. Larsen said.

Nancy took one more quick look around the yard, then turned back to Mrs. Larsen. "Thanks for letting us in," she said. "I've learned a lot."

"I'm so glad you came to investigate," Mrs. Larsen said. "Please do all you can to find out who's behind these awful burglaries. None of us feels safe. Reese is having a meeting for all the neighbors at his house on Sunday at noon to discuss how we can prevent future burglaries. Why don't you come to the meeting?"

"The day after tomorrow?" Nancy looked at George and Bess. They nodded. "Thanks. We'll be there."

They said goodbye and walked to the Mustang. "Want to bet the other two burgled families will be at that meeting?" George asked as Nancy put the key in the ignition and started the car. She backed out of the driveway.

Bess nodded, then looked sheepish. "How do you feel about triplets?"

"Why?" George asked, giving her a wary look.

"Because I promised Juanita we'd help her with the Kiley triplets' birthday party tomorrow afternoon," Bess explained.

"Wait—don't say anything, Nancy, I know you probably have all sorts of investigation plans, but at the Kileys' you'll get to see another house in River Estates with a Secure system. And you'll get to meet David. You'll even get to meet Diego the Great himself, because he'll be putting on a magic show for the party."

23

Nancy laughed as she drove down the street. "Looks like she managed to con us into baby-sitting again, George. Well, I need to talk to David," she said. "I'll drive you guys home now. Dad and Hannah are expecting me early for dinner. We'll meet for breakfast tomorrow, okay?"

"At the Waffle House," said Bess.

The next morning Nancy and Bess met George at the Waffle House. They each ordered blue-berry waffles. Right after the waiter left, Nancy heard a familiar voice. She looked around and saw Mrs. Mendenhall. She was sitting with a dark-haired man in a blue suit.

"You're my lawyer. Do something!" Mrs. Mendenhall was saying. "What about the city noise ordinance? You should have heard those kids when they were playing in the backyard yester-day. It's the same thing every Friday."

"I'm sorry, Alice," the lawyer replied. "Juanita doesn't need a license to operate a once-a-week play group for six kids. If she extends the group to every day and adds more kids, she could still get a license from the city. As long as she provides a safe environment for the kids—a fence and a clean house—there's nothing we can do."

"What about Juanita and her boyfriend rob-bing houses?" Mrs. Mendenhall said loudly.

Nancy winced, and Bess gasped. "What kind of child care provider is that?"

The lawyer murmured something Nancy couldn't hear. She looked around the room. All eyes were on Mrs. Mendenhall. It looked as if she might do anything she could to ruin Juanita's livelihood.

Bess shook her head. "What a rotten neighbor Juanita has."

After breakfast, Nancy drove Bess to the Kiley house, and George followed in her own car. The Kileys' front walk was paved with bricks and led to a roomy front porch full of white wicker furniture. Juanita met them at the door. "Come on in. These are Robbie, Corey, and Jamie Kiley," she said.

Three identical six-year-old boys dressed in jeans and red T-shirts stared up at Nancy, Bess, and George. They had curly blond hair and wide, innocent smiles.

"Hello, boys," Bess said as she knelt in front of them. "I'm Bess. Which one are you?" she asked the nearest triplet.

"I'm Jamie," he said sweetly.

"Now, Robbie," Juanita said, "it's not nice to try to confuse people. *This* is Jamie." She patted the head of one of the other boys.

"I'm Corey!" he said indignantly.

Juanita looked confused. "No, you're not, you're—"

"I'm Robbie, he's Corey!" The other triplet said with a grin.

Juanita looked helplessly at Nancy. "They've never done this before," she said. She shrugged her shoulders, then laughed. "I guess it doesn't matter." The boys laughed and ran around the living room, chasing one another.

Nancy motioned Juanita aside. "I need to ask you something," Nancy said. "Did you know any of the security codes at the burgled houses?"

"Of course not," Juanita said.

Nancy saw Bess close her eyes and turn away. Had Juanita forgotten about the Larsen code—or was she lying?

"Oh—wait," Juanita said. "I *did* know the Larsens' code. Melissa set off the alarm, and I had to punch in the numbers to shut it off." She shuddered. "You wouldn't believe how loud those alarms are."

Juanita's eyes widened. "So that's why the police suspect me! But I didn't know the Mowrers' or the Bairds' codes—honestly! I've never had to use the Larsen code again, and I swear I don't remember it."

Bess gave Nancy a relieved look and Nancy smiled. "I believe you," Nancy said quickly.

A little hand tugged at Nancy's sleeve. "I'm Robbie, and I have a bug jar." He held up a glass jar with a screened lid. "See? Will you help me catch some bugs outside?" he asked.

"Sure. But first we'd better see if Juanita needs help," Nancy said.

Bess waved her hand. "No, go ahead. George and I will watch Corey and Jamie."

"Right," George said. She rolled her eyes.

In the backyard Robbie turned over stones and looked under bushes. Finally he caught a cricket. He jumped up and down, excited, until Nancy gently took it from him and dropped it in the jar. Robbie ran off to find more bugs. Nancy screwed the lid back on the jar, then looked for Robbie. "Do you see any more?" she called. She looked around the yard. Where was Robbie?

"Stay calm," Nancy told herself. She looked behind the shrubs along the back porch, and behind the trees near the back gate. The gate was locked, so she moved along the fence, which was a sturdy chain-link one, about four feet high—too high for a little boy to climb over.

She stopped short. There was a hole in the fence, easily big enough for a little boy to climb through.

Nancy climbed over the fence. If Robbie had escaped and gone to the front yard, would he stay out of the street? Nancy ran to the front of the house.

Just as she reached the driveway, a green pick-up truck pulled up to the curb. A man dressed in black jumped out of the truck, startling Nancy.

Robbie scrambled out from under a forsythia bush, and the man ran up and grabbed him.

27

4

Abracadabra!

"Wait!" Nancy yelled. She raced up to the man and grabbed the back of Robbie's shirt. The man looked startled and for a moment stared warily back at Nancy as they both held on to the boy. Robbie looked over his shoulder at Nancy, his eyes wide.

"Who are you?" Nancy and the man said at the same time, glaring at each other.

"I'm Nancy Drew, and I'm baby-sitting this child," Nancy said.

The man looked relieved, then smiled. "Juanita told me you were helping her out— with baby-sitting and uh . . . the investigation," he said.

Nancy raised her eyebrows. "And you are?"

"Oh—sorry. I'm David Andrews, Juanita's boyfriend. I'm assisting with the magic show this afternoon," he explained. He hoisted Robbie onto his shoulders. Robbie giggled and held on to David's head.

Nancy studied David's face. His smile was warm as he looked up at Robbie, but his gaze slid away from Nancy when he saw her staring, and he looked embarrassed. His dark brown hair was curly and short on top but reached past his collar in the back. He was dressed in black jeans and a black sweatshirt.

David squinted into the sun, then back at Nancy. "So? Do I look like a thief?" he asked lightly.

Nancy blinked. "Sorry. No, you don't. But a lot of thieves don't look guilty, either," she said.

"I guess not. And you don't look much like a detective."

Nancy laughed. "Well, I hope I'm a better detective than I am a baby-sitter. I can't believe I lost Robbie so quickly."

David grinned. "Don't worry about it. Robbie's our little escape artist. You aren't the first person he's conned with that bug search routine. Want me to take him inside?" he asked.

Nancy waved David ahead of her, but instead of following them up the front steps, she headed to the backyard to examine the fence. She knew that a child could never have made that hole in the fence—it was too big.

She knelt down and ran her hands over the chain-link fence. The hole hadn't been caused by a tear. The cut was clean and straight, as if it had been made with wire cutters.

When Nancy stood up, she heard a rustle in the yard next door. A man was hunched over behind a bush, his back to her.

He raised a pair of binoculars and pointed them at the street in front of the Kiley house. He seemed to be looking at David's truck. Then he stood up and jogged around the side of the neighboring house, and was soon out of Nancy's sight.

Who was he? Could *he* have cut the fence?

Nancy made a note of what she'd seen in her notebook, then went into the Kiley house. The triplets were climbing on David.

"Make us disappear!" said one.

"Where's your magic hat?" asked another.

Juanita came up to Nancy and handed her some colorful paper plates. "Will you set the table, please?" she asked. "Mr. and Mrs. Kiley are at the bakery, getting the birthday cake."

Nancy took the plates. Juanita had paper streamers draped over her arms and was holding napkins and silverware in her hands. She set the table and pinned up the streamers, but she was always aware of what the children were doing.

"I don't know how anyone could accuse you of being a thief," Nancy said in a low voice. "Where would you find the time?"

"That's just it," Juanita said. "I couldn't. And

30

neither could David. He's either working at the Magic Shop or assisting at the shows. Grandfather says David will be a talented magician himself someday."

"I heard that," David said, coming up behind Juanita. "Don't you think I'm working hard enough, Nita?"

Juanita laughed. "You sound like Carlos."

"Speaking of working," Nancy said, "what happened at Secure, David? Why were you fired?"

He frowned. "Look—I really don't want to talk about it," he said.

"I've got to get started on the balloons," Juanita said. She left and went upstairs.

"But it was your job with Secure Monitoring that made you a suspect in the burglaries," Nancy said. "It's important for me to know why you were fired."

David ran a hand through his hair. "It doesn't matter, because you still wouldn't know anything about the burglaries," he said. "But I don't have alibis for them, so I can't prove I'm not involved."

"But you know the security codes in the houses that were robbed, don't you? You installed the systems," Nancy said.

"No—no! I don't know those security codes," David said, clenching his fist. "When I installed a system I tested it with the code once or twice,

31

but I didn't try to remember it—and I don't!" David glared at Nancy. "You're worse than the police."

Nancy shook her head. "I'm only trying to learn more about this case, David," she said. "Tell me, if I were a thief, how would I get into one of those houses without setting off the alarm?"

"I can't tell you that, Nancy," he said. "I signed a confidentiality agreement with Secure, promising not to reveal any information about their security equipment. Besides, those are top-of-the-line systems. The average thief would have a hard time getting past the motion detectors. You'd have to—" David stopped, and ran his hand through his hair again.

Nancy looked intently at David. "You'd have to what, David? Have the kind of information that only an employee of Secure could have?"

David turned and walked away, muttering something about getting ready for the magic show. Nancy sighed. If David were innocent, she thought, wouldn't he be more willing to answer her questions?

Juanita came back into the living room, holding a bunch of balloons. She began tying them to the chairs around the table.

"We're home!" Mr. and Mrs. Kiley came bustling through the front door, loaded with packages. "It looks lovely, Juanita!" Mrs. Kiley said.

"Here's the cake. Let's go into the kitchen and put on the candles."

It was close to one o'clock, so the party guests soon arrived as well. Children were dressed in their best clothes; the boys in neat shirts and slacks, and the girls in colorful dresses. Nancy caught her breath when a tall man with light brown hair walked in holding the hand of a dark-haired boy. It was the man she'd seen spying with the binoculars.

Nancy went over to Juanita, who was setting out plastic glasses on the party table, and pointed to the man.

"That's Reese Gardner and his son, Jimmy," Juanita said. "He's divorced, but he spends as much time as possible with Jimmy. He even gave him a birthday party not long ago." She looked at her watch. "It's so late! Come into the kitchen, Nancy. My grandfather should be arriving any minute."

So the man with the binoculars was Reese Gardner, Nancy thought. She wouldn't miss going to the meeting at his house tomorrow. "One more thing, Juanita," Nancy said, following her into the kitchen. "There's a hole in the chain-link fence outside. It looks like it was made with wire cutters."

Juanita looked puzzled. "Why would anyone cut the fence? I'll tell Mr. Kiley about it right away," she promised.

33

There was a quick knock on the back door, and Juanita hurried to open it. His arms full of equipment, Diego Puentes came into the kitchen. Nancy recognized him from the flyer.

"Good afternoon, Mr. Puentes," she said.

"Hello, Nancy Drew," Mr. Puentes answered cheerfully. "Please call me Diego—everyone does."

Nancy shook his hand, thinking that the warm look in his eyes no doubt charmed children as much as his magic tricks did.

A young man carrying a folded table followed Diego into the kitchen. He had coal black hair and blue eyes, and was dressed in black jeans and a black shirt. He smiled at Juanita. "Is David here yet?" he asked.

"He's in the living room," Juanita replied. Then she turned toward Nancy. "Nancy, this is Max Karn—he's my grandfather's new assistant. Max, meet Nancy Drew."

Max grinned at Nancy. "Hi, Nancy. I hope you're staying for the show."

"I wouldn't miss it," she said, smiling at him. Diego stacked some packages next to the door in the kitchen that led to the basement. Then he and Max headed down the hall with the table and the rest of the equipment, with Juanita and Nancy behind them.

In the living room, George and Bess were rounding up the children and seating them on

34

the floor to watch the magic show. Nancy started to sit down on a folding chair, then staggered and almost fell on the floor. Someone had jerked the chair out from under her. Carlos was holding on to the chair and grinning wickedly.

"Carlos," she said with a squeak, trying to get her breath back. "You could have hurt me. You're supposed to sit on the floor with the other kids."

"I'm a detective, too! See?" Carlos said. He pulled his notebook out from his pocket. "I want to sit in a chair like you."

Nancy looked down at Carlos, not sure whether to be annoyed or flattered. Juanita walked up and pointed to the floor. Carlos sat down and stuck out his bottom lip.

Nancy turned her attention to the center of the living room. Black sheets were hung over the windows to shut out the bright afternoon sun. Max and David stood behind the table, which was now draped with a dark cloth. "Ladies and gentlemen," David announced, "may I present—Diego the Great!"

Diego swept into the room, wearing a long silk cape and a black top hat, and carrying a black wand with a silver tip. He winked at his audience as the children cheered, then he nodded to Max. He turned off the lights, then shone a spotlight on Diego, who looked truly magical in the dark room.

Max went over to stand beside David at the

table. Diego put his top hat down, then looked at Max and frowned. "I don't need two assistants for this set of tricks," he said. He turned to the audience. "Shall I make one of them disappear?"

"Yes!" the children shouted. David handed Diego a black sheet. He draped it over Max's head, covering him completely. Diego tapped the top of the sheet with the magic wand and said, "Begone!" The sheet collapsed into a heap on the floor. The children gasped. Diego picked up the sheet and waved it.

Max must have ducked under the table, Nancy thought, behind the cloth. She was certain of it after Diego began to pull things from his top hat, which was still on the table—a pitcher of water, a live rabbit, and a long brass cane. Then he pulled out a dove, which spread its wings and flew around the room. The children squealed in delight, but Mrs. Kiley looked worried.

The dark room made the magic tricks look wondrous, and even Nancy was amazed when a white silk scarf pushed itself out of Diego's pocket. It grew longer and longer until it reached the top of Diego's head and wrapped itself into a turban.

Looking regal and mysterious, Diego turned to David. "What did you do with Max?"

"But, sir, you made him disappear!"

Diego frowned. "Well, now I need him again. Get him back—immediately!" he demanded.

"Yes sir," David said. He picked up the black sheet and held it behind the table. "Abracadabra and Kalamazoo—Max, I'd come back if I were you!"

The sheet rose slowly into the air. David snatched it aside. Max yawned and opened his eyes. "Where was I?" he said in a sleepy voice.

The children screamed and laughed in amazement. Max and David darted into the kitchen and came back pushing a tall cabinet with paneled doors. They placed it beside the table.

Diego opened both doors of the cabinet. It was empty. He motioned David inside, shut the doors, and waved his magic wand in front of the cabinet.

Diego opened the doors again. David was still inside, grinning. Diego turned to the audience with a surprised look on his face. "It didn't work!" he cried. He tilted his head and looked at the children. "Maybe if *you* said a magic word, it would work." Diego shut the doors again.

The children shouted, "Abracadabra!" Diego waved the wand, then threw open the doors of the cabinet. David was gone! The children cheered. Max turned the cabinet around. David was not behind it.

Nancy moved closer, took a good look, then exchanged glances with Bess and George. The cabinet was really empty.

Max stepped back against the wall, out of the

spotlight. Diego waved the magic wand with a flourish. "Now you children can answer a question for me. What's at the end of a rainbow?"

The children shouted, "A pot of gold!"

"Look!" Diego pointed to the ceiling with his wand. Colored lights were glowing and shifting, and finally formed into a shimmering rainbow. Nancy could see Max near a spotlight with revolving colored panes. Diego waved his wand, and a white light traveled along the arc of the rainbow to the side of the room. A golden pot shone in the light.

"Come, children," Diego said. "Let's gather around the pot to see what's inside." The children jumped up and ran to the pot. But when they looked inside, it was empty. Diego came up and shook his head. "Someone must be playing tricks on me. Who took my gold coins?"

He looked at the children, then his eyes grew wide. "There's one!" he cried. He snatched a gold coin from behind Robbie's ear. The children gasped. "It's real magic," said one of the boys. Then the children laughed as Diego discovered more gold coins, in their ears, under their chins, and behind their backs.

At last the lights came on. Diego held up three gold coins. "These magic coins are for the birthday boys—Robbie, Jamie, and Corey," he said. Diego handed each boy a shiny gold coin and wished him a happy birthday.

Nancy smiled as she looked at the delighted

faces of the children. Then she narrowed her eyes, studying each face. She realized she didn't remember seeing Carlos during the time Diego was pulling the magic coins out from around the children. That was strange. She stood up and looked around the room. Carlos was gone. Was he up to some new mischief?

Nancy dashed into the kitchen. It was empty. The birthday cake was on the counter—in one piece. Nancy breathed easier. But the basement door was open. She walked to the door and looked down the stairs into the dark basement.

She found the light switch, and was about to switch it on, when Carlos came clattering up the stairs toward her, his face white. "Someone's down there!" he yelled. "It's a burglar!"

5

Secrets at the Shop

Trembling, Carlos hugged Nancy's legs. Nancy looked down the basement stairs. "I don't see anyone," she said, patting his shoulder. "Why didn't you turn on the light?"

"It didn't work," Carlos said. "But *somebody's* down there!"

"I'll check it out," Nancy promised. She took Carlos back to the magic show, and he joined the other children, who were sitting down once again and watching Diego the Great perform.

Nancy grabbed her penlight from her purse and went back to the kitchen. Max was packing doves into his pockets from a cage by the basement door. He smiled and whispered, "Shh . . . don't tell the kids." His pockets full, he went into the living room.

Nancy opened the basement door and looked down the stairs. She flicked the light switch on the wall, but the lights didn't come on. She turned on her penlight and walked down the stairs.

She stepped slowly into the basement, which was full of shadows. Her feet hit something. Nancy stumbled, then fell down hard on the concrete floor.

She groaned and sat up. She shone her light on a tricycle. Baby-sitting can be dangerous indeed, she thought, looking at her arm.

She found a light switch and tried it. The lights came on, and she looked around. Both windows were shuttered, which was why the room had been so dark with the lights off. Nancy noticed a game table and shelves of games in the comfortably furnished room. She saw a Secure transmitter and remembered that Bess had said that the Kileys had a Secure system. She looked up at the wires, and followed them through the basement. The system looked just like the Larsens'.

Nothing in the basement seemed out of the ordinary, so Nancy went back upstairs. In the living room, David and Diego were packing up their equipment. The magic show was over. Mrs. Kiley was stacking presents in three separate piles. Carlos was holding gifts up to his ears and shaking them. "I'm helping you, Mrs. Kiley," he said.

Mr. Gardner was standing with some of the other parents. He turned and frowned at David. Why? Nancy wondered.

41

Max was talking to the triplets, smiling as they showed him the coins Diego had given them. They held the coins tightly and wouldn't even hand one to Max.

Max laughed as he knelt next to Robbie and his brothers. "Remember—don't try to spend them, or the magic will go away," Max said.

He stood up and looked at Nancy. "This is a great business—you know? Diego makes a lot of kids happy," he said.

"You and David were terrific, too," Nancy said.

"Thanks." He looked up as Diego called out his name. "I'm over here!" he yelled. "Well, see you later, Nancy—I have to help pack up the van."

Nancy found George helping Juanita set up a party game. "Can I talk to you a minute, George?" Nancy asked, and pulled her friends aside. "Did you see anyone leave the living room before I did?"

George frowned. "Sorry, Nancy, but I didn't even see you leave. Diego had me just as fascinated as the kids. He made David reappear in the cabinet, and Max did some tricks with doves. Then I had to help set up games for the kids," she said.

"Well, I'd better talk to Carlos," Nancy said. "I promised him I would check out the basement, but I'm sure he just imagined he saw someone."

Carlos was blindfolded and giggling as he played pin the tail on the donkey. The other

42

children were dancing around him, as he tried to attach the Velcro tail to Bess's hair.

When his turn was over, Carlos ran past Nancy. "Carlos—wait!" She stopped him in midflight by stepping in front of him. "I searched the basement but didn't see anyone," Nancy said. "Are you *sure* you saw someone?"

Carlos's eyes lit with excitement. "Yes—I'm sure," he said firmly. He pulled his notebook out of his pocket. Nancy saw a paper fall out of the notebook, but Carlos snatched it up and crammed it in his pocket.

He tapped the notebook with his pencil. "I was investigating a mystery, just like you do," he said, "but the light was broken. Then a burglar jumped at me! Or maybe it was a ghost—ghosts live in basements!"

"Thanks, Carlos." Nancy shook her head as he ran off again. It looked as if Carlos's wild imagination had sent her on a wild-goose chase.

After the triplets opened their presents, the cake and other refreshments were served. Soon after, the guests began to leave. Max and Diego had already left, but Nancy found David talking to Juanita.

Juanita smiled at Nancy. "Did you enjoy the show, Nancy?"

"I loved it—and I'd like to learn more about magic," Nancy said. She turned to David. "Do you think I could have a tour of the Magic Shop?"

43

"Sure," David said. "Why don't you and your friends come by about eleven o'clock tomorrow morning? I'll open the shop early."

"Sounds great. Thanks, David," Nancy said.

Nancy found Bess and George and told them about the Magic Shop tour set for the next morning. Afterward, they could drop by Reese Gardner's block watch meeting.

The next morning they met David at the Magic Shop. It was on Front Street, near the river. As David waved them through the door, Nancy looked around in wonder. The walls were covered with shelves, displaying items like top hats and odd-shaped boxes with false bottoms and trick doors. One shelf held collapsible birdcages and hat racks, designed to be folded almost flat and pulled out of a carpet bag.

"Wow," George said. "This place is incredible."

"Oh my gosh—look at this!" Bess rushed over to stare at a glowing green skull floating above a shelf. "How does it do that?" she asked David.

David grinned. "I can't reveal *all* our secrets. But come over here and I'll let you have a close look at a few tricks."

David picked up a stick. "This is a coin wand. Did you know that every time we handle a silver coin some of the silver wears off and is dispersed into the atmosphere," he said. "I'm sure you've all seen coins thin from wear. A coin wand collects the silver from the atmosphere."

David's eyes twinkled as he waved the wand in the air and a coin appeared at the end of it. Then he shook it over a box and Nancy heard it clatter into the box.

"It isn't really true—about the silver—is it?" Bess whispered to Nancy.

David laughed. "No, Bess, it isn't. This wand is operated by a battery," he said. "See, it has two slots on each side of the tip of the wand. A half coin is attached to a pivot in each slot. When I turn the switch on, the coin seems to leap off the wand, but with the switch off, the coin retreats into the wand and it looks like an ordinary plastic wand. The sound of a coin dropping off was made when I jiggled the box, which is already full of coins."

Nancy smiled. "You had me fooled. What about rope tricks? How do magicians escape when their hands are bound?" she asked.

David pulled out some rope. "Tie my hands, George," he ordered. He offered her his left wrist. George tied a tight loop around it. "Okay, now I'll turn around so you can tie my hands together behind my back."

David turned and crossed his right wrist across his left. George tied them together, stepping back as David turned around. He moved his hands briefly behind his back, then held up both hands, free of the rope.

David laughed at their expressions. He showed them how, when he'd turned his back, he had drawn one end of the rope through his fingers, creating a loop. Then he concealed the loop in his fist when he placed his right wrist over his left to be tied. Even after both hands were tied together, he could release enough slack to escape from the ropes.

"Hello, ladies!" Diego said, coming in from the back room. "What do you think of my shop?" he asked.

"It's fascinating," Nancy said.

The bell on the shop door rang. A man walked in and greeted Diego. His reddish brown hair was cut short and he wore a well-fitting navy blue suit.

"Hello, Ian," Diego said. He introduced the girls to Ian MacDonald, who was the owner of a magic supply shop in Hancock, to the south of River Heights. "What can I do for you?" Diego asked him.

"Well, I think I mixed up two of my orders," Mr. MacDonald said, "and may have given you the wrong bag of magic coins. Would you mind showing it to me? I'll exchange it for a new one."

"You know I've already given away some of the coins at my shows," Diego replied, "so it's not a new bag. I'll get it." Diego went into the back room.

Nancy walked up to a cabinet with panels that looked like the one David had disappeared from.

She stepped inside and felt along the back with her fingers. There didn't seem to be a hollow place at the back in which to hide.

She was still examining the inside of the cabinet when she heard Diego rush back into the room. "I've been robbed!" he shouted.

6

Caught in the Act

Nancy stepped out of the cabinet to see Diego pulling anxiously at his gray mustache. His voice was shaking. "The trunk where I keep the coins, and some props—it's empty!"

"Which props?" David asked, his hand on Diego's shoulder. "Maybe *I* moved them. I opened the storage trunk in here, but—"

"No, no," Diego said, shaking his head vigorously. "These were antique props from my grandfather's day. You wouldn't have needed them for anything. One is a small enchanted mirror, and the other is a crystal clock. The coins aren't valuable, of course, but the props are priceless."

Bess looked at Diego, her blue eyes wide. "Maybe the crooks who hit those houses in River Estates have decided to start robbing stores," she said.

"Diego doesn't have a Secure system," David said. He looked hopeful. "Maybe it's just a coincidence that the burgled houses had Secure systems. The police have me pegged as a thief because of my connection with Secure. Maybe this will convince them I might be innocent."

"You'd better check the cash register," George suggested. "If someone robbed the place, they'd take what's in the cash register, too, wouldn't they?"

"Are you sure they took *all* the coins you bought?" Mr. MacDonald asked Diego.

Diego nodded his head sadly as he opened the cash register. "I had to lock up the coins because my grandson kept taking them—I was afraid he'd lose them." He checked the register drawer. "There's nothing missing. But, then, who took—"

"Wait!" Nancy said firmly. "Let's make sure there's actually been a robbery. Can you show me the trunk?"

Diego led the way into the back room. Boxes were stacked on metal shelves along three walls. Along the wall by the door were four wooden trunks with brass locks. "I keep my most valuable equipment in these trunks," Diego said.

Nancy knelt by a trunk that had its lid open. She examined the old-fashioned lock and the front of the trunk. She looked up at Diego. "There are a few scratches around the lock, but

49

nothing looks pried open. It must have been opened with a key," she said.

"Impossible," Diego said. "I keep the keys on my belt. See?" He held up a chain with brass keys dangling from it.

Bess knelt next to Nancy. "Look—there are scratches on this trunk, too." She turned to the third trunk. "And this one."

"Someone's been trying to open these trunks," Nancy said. "Do you always have the keys on you, Diego? Even at home with Juanita and Carlos?"

"Carlos!" David hit his forehead with his hand. "I saw Carlos playing with some keys last night when he and Juanita stopped by. He left here with a bulging backpack. I thought it was full of his toys," he said.

Diego hurried to the phone and called Juanita. Moments later his booming laugh rang out through the shop. He hung up the phone. "I wasn't robbed after all! That wily little grandson of mine had the mirror and the clock on a shelf in his room," he said.

"But how did he get into the trunk?" George asked.

Diego laughed again. "He said he found the keys, and you know—he's right. I took them off my belt last night and left them on the kitchen table while I tried on costumes for the magic act. He must have picked them up and then returned them when Juanita brought him home. She didn't find the coins, but the props are what's valuable. I can always get more coins, right, Ian?"

Mr. MacDonald cleared his throat. "Yes, of course," he said. "I'll check with you later. I'd better get back to my store." He smiled and left.

Nancy, George, and Bess chatted with Diego for a few minutes, then said goodbye.

As she followed Nancy and George out of the shop, Bess stared at the glowing green skull. "This place is a little creepy," she said.

They climbed into the Mustang, and Nancy drove them to River Estates. They were late for the meeting at Reese Gardner's house, which was scheduled to start at noon. Late or not, Nancy didn't want to miss the opportunity to talk to the owners of the two other burgled houses, the Bairds and the Mowrers.

Mr. Gardner's house had dark brown siding and a decorative glass window in the front door. He looked surprised to see the young women when he answered the door. "Look, I'm busy—" he began.

"Mrs. Larsen invited us," Nancy interrupted, craning her head to see past him into the foyer. "Oh—there she is! Hello, Mrs. Larsen—sorry we're late."

Frowning, Mr. Gardner held open the door. Mrs. Larsen came up and introduced Nancy and her friends to Mr. Gardner. He led them through the front hall, then into a living room furnished with leather couches and folding chairs. People

51

were milling about, talking to one another. Officer Brody was near the fireplace, looking over the crowd. The meeting hadn't started yet, it seemed. Nancy asked Bess to find and interview the Mowrers. George volunteered to talk to other people about burglaries in case they knew something of interest.

Nancy walked up to Mr. Gardner, who was at the refreshment table. "I'd like to know what you think about the burglaries," she said.

"I've already talked to the police about it," he said.

"Do you happen to have a Secure Monitoring system, too?" she asked him.

He shrugged. "Almost everyone in River Estates has a Secure system—they're the best in town." He rearranged some silverware on the table.

Deciding to be more direct, Nancy tried again. "Mrs. Larsen told me she gave you her security code when you fed her cat. I was wondering if this was a common practice among neighbors. Have you given your code to anyone?"

"I must tell you I resent your prying," Mr. Gardner said angrily. "I'm sure the police can handle this investigation without help from *amateurs.*"

"I'm only trying to help," Nancy said.

Mr. Gardner didn't respond. He turned away and clapped his hands. "People, take your seats. Time to begin."

Nancy found a seat and looked around. She'd hoped to see the Kileys, but Mrs. Larsen had told her they were at a family reunion and wouldn't be back until the next day.

Officer Brody went to the front of the room, and began to speak. "There's a great deal ordinary citizens can do to protect their property," he said. "One way is to set up a block watch. Neighbors take turns watching each other's houses for suspicious vehicles in the vicinity, among other things." He spoke for another ten minutes, then asked for questions. Nancy held up her hand. He frowned and called on someone else. Nancy gave a mental shrug. Officer Brody had better get used to seeing her—she was going to solve this case.

Most of the residents were eager to begin a block watch and asked a lot of questions, which Officer Brody answered patiently. Nancy listened carefully and was able to learn many of the residents' names.

At last the discussion ended. Nancy got up and walked over to the Bairds and introduced herself. Mrs. Baird was a slim woman with red hair pulled back in a French braid. "Do you know how the thieves got into your house?" Nancy asked.

"Yes, through our upstairs bedroom window," Mrs. Baird said. "It was such a shock to come home to a burglary. But they didn't touch my jewelry."

"The thieves stole only a few items, including our VCR," Mr. Baird added. His dark blond hair was cut short. "Our daughter, Amy, is certain she's missing some things, too. But you know how kids' rooms are." He shook his head. "But they took my coin collection."

"Was it valuable?" Nancy asked.

He shrugged. "Sometimes the value of a coin depends on how many collectors want it to complete a collection," he explained. "Only a few of my coins were worth over five hundred dollars."

Mr. Baird grimaced. "But I was especially sorry to lose my Liberty coins," he said. "My 1921 Walking Liberty and Mercury coins were part of a Lady Liberty collection I'm trying to build."

Mr. Baird sighed and put his arm around Mrs. Baird. "I was planning to buy one of the most beautiful Liberty coins ever produced," he added. "It's a 1911 twenty-dollar gold piece designed by the Irish-American sculptor Augustus Saint-Gaudens. Lady Liberty is portrayed in a flowing gown with a lot of detail."

"It sounds beautiful. I hope the police locate your collection," Nancy said. "Excuse me. I have to find my friends."

Nancy motioned to Bess and George, and they came over to talk to her. George had spoken to several residents and Officer Brody. The residents were baffled and alarmed, and the police had no leads on the stolen items.

Bess was beaming. "I found out a lot. The Mowrer robbery sounds a lot like the Larsen robbery," she said. "An upstairs window was pried open, but the thieves ignored the expensive jewelry in the bedroom. They went downstairs and ransacked the kids' rooms, then took just a TV set and a laptop computer."

"Some toys are also missing," Bess continued, "and Mrs. Mowrer said their daughter is missing a coin she had in her room. There were dog tracks, too, just like at the Larsens'. Don't you think the same thief must be robbing all these houses?"

"Sounds like it," Nancy said. "Were the Mowrers' upstairs windows unwired, too?"

Bess nodded. "But the motion detectors were on, and Secure Monitoring Company said that nothing was wrong with their system."

George shook her head. "So we have a thief who enters through upstairs windows and can defeat a top-of-the-line security system. But instead of stealing obvious expensive items, he ransacks kids' rooms, takes toys and TVs, and brings his dog along?"

Nancy sighed. "Sounds ridiculous, doesn't it? Well, we know that Juanita doesn't own a dog and David probably doesn't, either."

As Nancy noticed Reese Gardner going into the kitchen, she wondered, Why had he been spying on David's truck? Was he the one who cut the Kileys' fence to get a quick way into and out of the backyard—maybe for a future burglary? He *had* known the security code at the Larsen house, making him a suspect. He was definitely worth checking on, she decided.

Nancy turned back to Bess and George. "See if you can distract Mr. Gardner while I check out the basement, okay?" she asked. "I think the door is in the hall. I want to see if he has any heavy-duty wire cutters."

George and Bess headed for the kitchen. The basement door was in the hall, as Nancy had suspected. She opened it quietly and went down the stairs, closing it behind her. She searched among the tools on Mr. Gardner's workbench. No wire cutters.

Nancy looked up and noticed security system wires. She followed the wires through the basement and saw wired window bars like the ones in the Larsen house. The systems seemed identical.

She stepped back, looking up to find the transmitter. Then she froze. She'd heard a sound behind her, like someone breathing. Then a hand gripped her shoulder—hard.

Nancy gasped and whirled around. Reese Gardner was glaring at her, his face red and furious. "What are you doing in my basement, Nancy Drew?"

7

Alarming Circumstances

Nancy looked into Reese Gardner's angry green eyes. "Um . . . I thought I saw Mr. Baird come down here," she said. She looked around innocently. "But I guess he didn't."

Nancy dodged around Mr. Gardner and headed for the stairs. He followed her up. Nancy could feel his eyes boring into her back.

Upstairs, people were leaving. Bess came up to Nancy and whispered, "Sorry, but Mr. Gardner escaped from the kitchen. Did he catch you in the basement?"

Nancy grinned. "He sure did. But it doesn't matter. I didn't find anything," Nancy said. "Let's get George and go to Juanita's to fill her in about the meeting."

Nancy drove to Juanita's house and parked the car. Mrs. Mendenhall was in her driveway, loading a boxy black item into the trunk of her car.

Nancy remembered Mrs. Mendenhall's call to the police about David and her conversation with her lawyer.

"Follow me," Nancy whispered to Bess and George. They went over to Mrs. Mendenhall's car, then stopped short. Mrs. Mendenhall was bent over, trying to fit a portable TV in the trunk next to two VCRs and a laptop computer. Nancy remembered the stolen goods she'd heard about at the meeting. Could Mrs. Mendenhall be the burglar? She worked nights—so did burglars— and she had a dog. Could she be trying to frame Juanita and David to divert suspicion from herself?

George leaned over Nancy's shoulder. Bess craned her neck to see past George. Mrs. Mendenhall straightened up and stared at the trio, a hostile look on her face.

"Oh, a laptop computer," George said. "My dad has one just like that."

Mrs. Mendenhall slammed the trunk shut. "Isn't that nice," she snapped. Mrs. Mendenhall cocked her head at Nancy. "Hasn't the great detective solved the burglaries in the ritzy neighborhood yet?"

"Not yet," Nancy said, "but we just came from a block watch meeting at Mr. Gardner's house. Maybe future burglaries can be prevented."

Mrs. Mendenhall chuckled. "At Gardner's house—that's a laugh," she said. "He's the one with a criminal record."

"What do you mean?" Nancy asked quickly.

"It's not *my* business," Mrs. Mendenhall said, getting into her car. "But I read the papers. That's why his wife divorced him." She started the car and drove off.

"What's that supposed to mean?" George asked.

"Do you think Mr. Gardner really has a criminal record?" Bess asked as they walked up Juanita's driveway.

"I don't know," Nancy said. "Would you and Bess try to find out tomorrow? Check the newspapers at the library."

"Do you think that stuff in Mrs. Mendenhall's trunk was stolen?" Bess asked.

"It could have been," Nancy replied. "Mrs. Mendenhall has now become a suspect. Why else would she try to blame Juanita and David?"

They reached the porch and George asked, "Isn't that guy talking to Carlos the one we met in the magic shop this morning?"

As they came up the steps Ian MacDonald smiled. "Uh . . . Nancy, Bess, and George— right?" he asked. "I was hoping Carlos could tell me where Diego was."

Carlos grabbed Nancy's hand. "Come see my treasure!" Like a puppy on a leash, he pulled her around to the backyard. He dropped her hand, then crawled under a bush. He dragged out a bag and opened it, and a mass of gold coins spilled onto the ground.

Nancy bent down and picked up a coin. Magic Coin was written on it in small letters. So David had been right, Nancy thought. Carlos had taken the bag of coins along with the mirror and clock.

Mr. MacDonald knelt down next to Carlos. "Let me help you pick those up, Carlos," he said. "That's quite a treasure you have there."

"No! They're mine!" Carlos said. He threw himself down on top of the coins, covering them. Mr. MacDonald looked annoyed.

"Carlos!" Juanita came out of the back door. "I saw you. Why did you take those coins again? Grandfather needs them for the magic show." She pulled Carlos to his feet, then scooped up the coins and put them into the bag.

"Here"—Juanita dug her hand into the bag— "you can keep one, okay?"

Carlos took the coin. "Can I have one more?" he asked.

Juanita shook her head and turned to Ian MacDonald. "Hello, Mr. MacDonald. If you're looking for my grandfather, he's still at the Magic Shop."

"Thanks, I'll check there," he said, dusting the grass off his knees. He walked toward the front of the house, and almost collided with David, who was coming around the corner. They greeted each other, then David waved at Juanita and walked up to her.

"Hi, David," Juanita said. "Here are the coins.

If you drive me to the shop, Carlos can return them." She turned to Nancy. "So, how did the block watch meeting go?" she asked. "Did you find out anything that might help clear David and me?"

"I'm sorry, Juanita," Nancy said. "All the burglaries followed the same pattern; the thief must have had some inside knowledge of the security systems." She looked at David.

David narrowed his eyes. "You mean me! I know how the systems work—right?"

"David, calm down," Juanita said quietly.

"Why should I be calm?" he asked. "Your so-called friend is trying to put me in jail!"

Juanita whispered something to David and pulled him out front, with Carlos following them. David threw Nancy an angry look over his shoulder. "You'd better not pin those burglaries on me," he said.

"Was that a threat?" George asked softly.

"I don't know," Nancy said. "But I'd love to search David's truck."

"Can it wait?" Bess asked. "I'm hungry."

"Want to come over to my house?" Nancy asked. "Hannah's baking a ham for Sunday dinner."

"Fabulous!" George said.

A short while later, they were seated around the table. Nancy's father, Carson Drew, carved the ham, and the platter of slices made the rounds, followed by baked sweet potatoes and Brussels sprouts.

Hannah, the Drews' housekeeper, spooned some gravy over her ham, and asked, "How are things going with your case, Nancy?"

Mr. Drew speared a slice of ham with his fork. "What did you find out at the block watch meeting?" he asked.

Nancy told her father and Hannah what had happened at the meeting. "We also found out," she said, "that the burglars got into the houses through windows on the second floor, which weren't wired into the security system."

Bess waved her fork, and said, "I asked Mrs. Mowrer why her upstairs windows weren't wired. She said it costs a lot to wire just the downstairs and the basement. And if you *did* wire the upstairs windows, they couldn't be opened at night."

"Even though the windows weren't wired," George added, "there are motion detectors on the stairways, which are supposed to set off the alarm. The weird thing is, the thieves did go downstairs and take things, but the alarms didn't go off."

"Don't forget," Bess said, "when the police arrived, the systems weren't even on. So Secure Monitoring said the owners forgot to activate them in the first place. But *all* the homeowners insisted they didn't forget. Which means that the intruder must have known how to shut down the system. Or, if he somehow learned the security code—"

"Maybe from feeding a neighbor's cat?" George put in.

"Oh, right!" Bess said. "Mrs. Larsen gave Mr. Gardner her code so he could feed her cat."

"That's it!" Nancy said. She pushed her plate away and leaned forward. "The burglar could break in upstairs through the unwired window, and if he knew the security code, he could punch in the code on the upstairs control panel. That would shut off the motion detectors, and then he could move freely through the house."

"Are you saying Mr. Gardner is a suspect?" Mr. Drew asked. Hannah stood up and began to clear the table.

Nancy nodded. "So is a woman named Alice Mendenhall. She's Juanita's neighbor, and we just saw her loading a bunch of TVs and VCRs into her trunk—that makes her a suspect, too." Nancy handed Hannah her plate.

"But why did the thief ignore expensive items, yet always ransack the kids' rooms? And why take toys from the backyard?" George asked. She picked up her plate and Bess's and took them into the kitchen. Bess stood up and finished clearing the table.

Mr. Drew arched an eyebrow. "Toys? That *is* strange," he remarked. "You told me the police

63

consider David Andrews a suspect. Couldn't he shut down the systems *without* the codes, since he installed them?"

"Probably," Nancy agreed, "I wish I knew more about security systems."

Mr. Drew looked thoughtful. Hannah came back with a pot of coffee and pie plates. Bess was right behind her with a homemade apple pie, Mr. Drew's favorite dessert.

After the coffee was poured and pieces of pie passed around, Mr. Drew said, "You know, a friend of mine, Joel Gordon, lives in River Estates. He has a Secure Monitoring system. Maybe I could arrange for you to have a good look at it."

"That would be a big help," Nancy said.

After dinner, Nancy's father called Mr. Gordon, who suggested they come over right away, since he was catching a plane that evening to go on a business trip.

"Let's go," Nancy said. The three girls dashed out of the house.

It wasn't long before Mr. Gordon was standing with Nancy, George, and Bess at his security control panel. "I'm programming a temporary code into the keypad," he told them. "This way I don't have to tell you my real code." That's what Mrs. Larsen should have done with Mr. Gardner, Nancy thought.

Mr. Gordon showed Nancy how to test the system to see whether it was working. "A three-tone signal will beep if the windows are opened or if the motion detectors sense movements," he told her. "But this is only a test. If it were for real, the alarm would go off, and the alarm code would appear on Secure Monitoring's computers. Then Secure would call the police."

Nancy looked at the control panel. "What would happen if someone cut the wires or tried to disable the system at the control panel? Would the alarm let Secure know?"

Mr. Gordon nodded and looked at his watch. "I'm sorry, but time's running short. Take a closer look while I go next door. My neighbor said he'd watch my house while I was gone, and I have to give him the key." Mr. Gordon left the house.

Nancy put the alarm on test mode. Together with Bess and George, she walked through the house, located the motion detectors, then listened to the tones as they moved around the rooms.

They also discovered that even when George crawled along the floor, the tones would sound. Nancy went back to the upstairs control panel and turned on the system, but not the motion detectors, so they could move around freely. Then they went down to the basement.

Nancy's eyes followed the wires around and above the windows and throughout the basement. Mr. Gordon's system looked just like the Larsens'. Then she stopped short. A rolled-up paper was taped to one of the wires near a window. She stood on tiptoe but couldn't reach it.

George dragged over a box and stood on it. "I can reach it, Nancy," she said. But just as George's hand touched the paper, she leaned over too far and her foot slipped off the box.

George grabbed the bar on the window for balance. A deafening scream filled the basement as sirens blared inside and outside the house. George had set off the alarm.

8

Date with a Doberman

Bess clapped her hands over her ears. "George, what did you do?" she yelled.

George shook her head helplessly and jumped off the box. The sirens continued to blare.

Nancy raced up the basement staircase, with George and Bess after her. At the control panel, Nancy frantically tried to remember the temporary code.

"It was six, eight, five, uh . . . two!" George yelled.

"No it wasn't!" Bess shouted, as the sirens continued to blare. "It was six, five, eight . . ."

Nancy fumbled in her pocket with shaking hands. She found the slip of paper where she'd written down the code. "Six, five, two, eight . . . I've got it!" she cried, and punched in the numbers.

The alarm stopped and a delightful silence fell

over the house. "Ohhh . . ." Bess moaned, "my ears are still ringing."

Mr. Gordon rushed through the open door. "What's going on here?" he cried.

Nancy stared at the control panel. Then she heard another siren wailing. Tires screeched on pavement. Car doors slammed.

The front door burst open, and Officer Brody and another policeman ran in, guns drawn.

Bess gasped and put up her hands.

Officer Brody stopped short. "We were just down the block when we heard the alarm. We were hoping we'd catch the crooks in the act," he said. "What are you doing here, Nancy?"

"Mr. Gordon was kind enough—" Nancy began.

George winced. "I'm sorry," she said to Mr. Gordon. "I accidentally set off your alarm."

Mr. Gordon sighed in relief. "I can vouch for these ladies," he told Officer Brody. "I was showing them my security system. Now, if you don't mind, I have a plane to catch."

The next morning Nancy brought her notes up to date. As she wrote about the events of the previous evening, she realized that she'd completely forgotten the rolled-up paper on Mr. Gordon's security wires. She hadn't seen papers like that on the wires at the other houses. She went to the phone and called Secure Monitoring Company. A salesman answered.

"Hello," Nancy said cheerfully. "I wondered if you could give me some information on your systems."

"How big is your house?" the salesman asked.

"I'm not in the market for a system," Nancy said. "I want to know about a paper I saw rolled up and taped to the wires of my friend's alarm system. Can you tell me if the paper was put there by Secure, and what could be on it?"

The man's voice at the other end of the line was guarded. "I can't give out information like that," he said.

"Well, maybe you could answer another question," Nancy said. "Do you know why one of your installers—his name is David Andrews—was fired?"

"I'm sorry, but I cannot give out information like that," he repeated, and hung up.

Nancy made a face, then replaced the receiver. That was a wasted phone call. Why wouldn't the man discuss the rolled-up paper with her? If only she'd remembered to check it the night before, but there'd been too much confusion and not enough time.

The phone rang and broke her train of thought. It was Bess, who told her about an arts and crafts exhibit at Sycamore Park.

"It sounds like fun," Nancy said.

"Great," Bess said. "George and I have a lot to tell you, and we need to stop at Juanita's, too. Can you pick us up at my house?"

Ten minutes later Nancy picked up Bess and George. They scrambled into the car.

"Oh, Nancy, do we have news!" George said when Nancy drove off. "Bess and I checked out Reese Gardner's criminal record at the library this morning."

"Is it true that he has one?" Nancy asked.

"Does he!" she said. "According to the newspaper articles I read, Mr. Gardner was convicted five years ago of embezzling from the investment firm where he worked."

Bess nodded rapidly. "Then I found out that he got out of prison early for good behavior."

Nancy bit her lip, thinking hard. "It seems doubtful that an embezzler would start burgling houses." She pulled the car over to the curb and parked. "We're here," she said, and they piled out.

Bess grabbed Nancy's arm. "Oh, look!" she cried. "A hot dog vendor! I'm starved." She dashed over to the hot dog cart. When Nancy and George reached her side, a young man was smearing mustard on a hot dog for Bess.

"Aren't you Max Karn?" Nancy asked, looking closely at the vendor's face. "Diego's assistant?"

Max grinned and nodded, pointing at his white hat. "I work a lot of odd jobs," he said. "So you could say I wear a lot of different hats."

"Diego doesn't need you every day?" Nancy asked.

"Most of our magic shows are at birthday

parties, and they tend to take place on week-ends," Max replied. He waved at his cart. "How about a footlong with the works?"

"Try one, they're wonderful," Bess said with her mouth full. "I need a soda."

Nancy and George bought hot dogs and sodas and said goodbye to Max. They walked around the exhibit for a while. George and Bess finished their hot dogs and sodas, but Nancy wasn't that hungry. She drank her soda but didn't finish her hot dog. "I'll eat it later," she said. When they got back to the Mustang, Nancy handed George the hot dog to hold for her.

Nancy drove to Juanita's house and parked. As she climbed out of the car, she heard Buster growling in the yard next door. Nancy went up to the fence and peered over. Buster was growling and chewing on a plastic toy.

"What's that he's chewing on?" George asked.

"It looks like a toy fire truck. The kids must have thrown it over the fence," Nancy said, sighing. "Maybe we'd better take it away from him."

"What?" Bess gasped, staring at Nancy. "Have you lost your mind? Buster'll eat us for lunch! He could—"

"Now, Bess," Nancy said. "We have to get that toy away from him, or Mrs. Mendenhall will make more trouble for Juanita. George, give Bess my hot dog, and I'll zip over there and get the toy. Okay?"

71

"I don't know . . ." Bess said, her voice trailing off uncertainly.

"I'll back you up," George said, handing Bess the hot dog.

Buster raised his head. The hair along his neck rose. He dropped the truck and growled, keeping his eyes on them.

"Here, Buster," Bess cooed. "Look at the nice hot dog." Buster looked up and sniffed.

"That's right—keep his attention," Nancy whispered. She looked at the fence. It was about four feet tall. A few large rocks and bushes near the foot of the fence might provide an easy way over it.

Bess nervously waved the hot dog at Buster while Nancy looked for a place to climb over the fence. Buster stopped growling and trotted over to Bess, sniffing.

Nancy climbed onto a rock, then vaulted over the fence. She scooped up the fire truck and threw it over the fence into Juanita's yard. "Yuck," she said, and wiped her fingers on her jeans.

"Hurry, Nancy," Bess whispered, dangling the hot dog above Buster's head and trying to break a piece from it. Buster leaped at her hand. She squealed and dropped a piece of the hot dog, which he gobbled. "This was a terrible idea—I could lose a finger. Hurry!"

Nancy knew she had to get out of the yard fast, but she'd seen something small and red in the doorway of the doghouse and headed for it. Another plastic truck. Holding it in her hand, she got down on her knees and peered into the doghouse. A pile of toys was stashed in a corner.

Oh no, she thought. She hated the idea of crawling into the doghouse.

Nancy took a deep breath, then crawled to the back of the doghouse. She scooped up the toys and backed out.

Bess screamed. "Nancy—I ran out of hot dog!"

"He sees you, Nancy! Run!" George yelled.

Nancy ran partway to the fence, threw the toys over into Juanita's yard, and headed toward a garden shed, which was closer. Buster's growl was right behind her. She picked up speed.

Her foot hit the handle of a shovel, and she tripped and fell through the doorway of the shed. Bess was still screaming. Nancy felt Buster's paws slam against her back, pinning her down.

She turned over and saw Buster's teeth in her face, saliva dripping from his jaws.

He growled and lunged for her throat.

9

Robbed!

"Nancy!" George yelled. She backed up a bit, then ran forward and jumped over the fence. She was holding a metal trash can lid. She raced to the shed, ready to do battle with Buster.

But Buster had stopped growling and was licking Nancy's face. Buster whined softly, and wagged his tail. Nancy sucked in her breath, wondering if she could breathe with Buster's weight on her.

Nancy let out her breath, then turned her head, trying to escape his slobbering jaws. Buster kept licking her face as if she were a puppy. Out of the corner of her eye, Nancy saw Bess collapse, shaking, against the fence. George stood outside the shed, staring, her trash can shield still in her hand. "Nancy?" she asked. "Are you okay?"

Mrs. Mendenhall stormed out the back door in her pajamas. "Just what do you girls think you're

74

doing?" she yelled. "Who said you could play with my dog? Buster's a watchdog—not a playmate! Release him immediately!"

"Uh . . . I'd love to, but . . ." Nancy slipped one hand out from under Buster to wipe her wet face. "He doesn't seem to want to move," she said.

Mrs. Mendenhall marched over to Buster and yanked on his collar. "Off, Buster!" she demanded.

Buster jumped off Nancy and ran to Mrs. Mendenhall. Nancy staggered to her feet, and her elbow hit something hanging on the wall near the door.

A pair of heavy-duty wire cutters was hanging from a hook. "Look," Nancy said.

George nodded. "They look strong enough to cut through the Kileys' chain-link fence," she said.

George and Nancy walked through the gate, which Mrs. Mendenhall held open for them, still scolding them for playing with Buster.

Bess put her hand on Nancy's shoulder. "I thought Buster was going to *eat* you!"

Nancy rubbed her face with her hands, then sniffed. "Ugh. I smell like Buster," she said. "But we found out"—she lowered her voice—"that Mrs. Mendenhall owns a pair of heavy-duty wire cutters. She could have cut the Kileys' fence."

Nancy, George, and Bess walked over to Juanita's house. "What was Mrs. Mendenhall yelling about?" Juanita asked when she let them in. George told her about Buster and showed her the toys.

Juanita picked up a slimy car. "Yuck . . . Well, I'm happy to say that none of these is mine."

"Maybe they belong to the kids who live on the other side of Mrs. Mendenhall," George said.

Juanita shook her head. "No kids live there."

"That's strange," Nancy said. "I've got to wash my hands and face. Is it okay if I use the kitchen sink?"

Juanita handed her a bar of soap and a towel. "Be my guest."

While Nancy washed up, Juanita and Bess talked quietly. Then Juanita said, "Nancy, George, I hate to ask . . . but would you help me with one more baby-sitting job?"

"You'll love it," Bess said.

Nancy and George looked at each other. "We should have known," George said. "Okay, where is it?"

"At the skating rink. Four o'clock this afternoon," Juanita said. "I promised to take the play group roller-skating."

"And I told Juanita that she had to ask you herself. I didn't want to spring it on you," Bess said.

Nancy smiled at Juanita. "We'll be there." She'd noticed an open psychology book on the table. "We'd better go and let you study," she said.

On the way to the Mustang, Nancy heard George moaning under her breath about baby-sitting again. Nancy wasn't looking forward to it, either—Carlos would probably be there, and Carlos was always trouble. On the other hand, Juanita was working hard, and she needed all the help she could get.

"What's next, Nancy?" Bess opened the door of the car.

Nancy got behind the wheel. "I think we should tail Reese Gardner. We can't ignore the fact that he has a criminal record," she said.

Nancy drove the short distance to River Estates. The neighborhood was quiet; most people were still at work. A car was parked in the Gardner driveway. "Looks as if he's home," said George.

Nancy parked the Mustang across the street. "Let's hope he goes somewhere," she said.

After watching the house for fifteen minutes, Bess yawned and slumped back in the seat. "This is so boring, Nancy," she said. "What if he's taking a nap or something?"

"Shh . . . there he is," Nancy said. Mr. Gardner locked the door behind him and walked toward his car. "Duck!" Nancy said.

A moment later Nancy heard his car start and drive away. Three heads popped up cautiously, then Nancy started the Mustang and headed after Mr. Gardner. She tried to keep a good distance behind him, with at least one car between them.

Mr. Gardner drove downtown and parked a few stores away from the Magic Shop.

"That's strange," Nancy said, pulling the Mustang over across the street. "He didn't turn his engine off or get out of the car; he's just sitting there."

A few minutes later, David came out of the Magic Shop. He got into his truck and drove off.

"There goes Mr. Gardner," said George.

"He's following David," said Bess.

Nancy pulled the Mustang out into the traffic, keeping a couple of cars between her and Mr. Gardner. She was perplexed. *They* were following Mr. Gardner, and *he* was following David.

It wasn't long before Nancy realized David was headed toward Juanita's neighborhood. Finally, he stopped his truck in front of Juanita's house. Mr. Gardner stopped, too, and parked behind a row of shrubs on the corner. Nancy pulled over behind a parked car on the other side of the street.

By this time David was going into Juanita's house. Mr. Gardner hurried out of his car and ran over to David's truck. He looked in the side storage compartments in the back of the truck. Then he peered through the window.

Nancy heard a screen door slam just as Mr. Gardner reached for the door handle. Carlos skipped into view and stopped short when he saw Mr. Gardner. Nancy quietly opened the door of the Mustang. What would Mr. Gardner do when he saw Carlos?

Mr. Gardner backed quickly away from Carlos, climbed back into his car, and drove away.

Bess jumped out of the Mustang and caught up with Carlos, who was dragging his bicycle from the bushes. "Carlos!" Bess cried. "You know Juanita doesn't want you to ride your bike without a helmet."

Nancy slapped the steering wheel in frustration. Reese Gardner's car had turned the corner. There was no point in chasing after him now.

"I wasn't going far," Carlos said, biting his lip.

"Bess," Nancy said between clenched teeth, "why don't you take Carlos into the house so he can get his helmet."

"Come on, Carlos," Bess said, holding out her hand. He took it, and they went back into the house.

"That Carlos," George said. "He keeps turning up, like a bad penny."

Nancy relaxed. "Might as well make the most of it," she said, and got out of the Mustang.

"I wonder what Mr. Gardner was looking for," George said as she climbed out of the car.

"I don't know," Nancy said, "but I want to get a good look at David's truck. The last time I saw David, he lost his temper and practically threatened me. Maybe Mr. Gardner knows something about David that I don't."

Nancy walked over to the truck. She could see some magic props lying in the back of the truck, along with emergency road equipment. Nancy looked through the window and saw the end of a rope sticking out from under the front seat. She opened the door slowly, wincing when a rusty hinge let out a loud squeak.

Nancy pulled on the rope. It turned out to be a long, lightweight rope ladder. She held it and wondered whether someone could use a rope ladder to climb into a house.

A voice behind her made her jump. "What are you doing, Nancy?" David asked.

Nancy turned. David was holding a crowbar and glaring at her. She flashed him a sheepish look, cleared her throat, and said, "Uh, I was wondering—why do you have a rope ladder?"

David studied her face. "If you must know," he said, "I'm trying out a new trick based on an Indian rope-climbing illusion. That length of ladder should be perfect for it."

"And the crowbar?" Nancy asked.

David's mouth tensed into a straight line. "Look, Juanita asked me to pry open a stuck cabinet door. Why don't you ask her if you don't believe me," he said angrily.

"It's not that I don't believe you—" Nancy began. Sirens wailing, a group of police cars rushed by. "That's Officer Brody," George said. "He's headed toward River Estates!"

"See you later, David," Nancy said. Bess ran

out of Juanita's house. Nancy waved her toward the Mustang. "Let's follow Officer Brody," Nancy said. "It could be another burglary."

Following the wail of the sirens, Nancy drove to River Estates. "There they are," George said. Nancy parked behind the police cars in front of the Kileys' house and dashed up to Officer Brody. He was leaning on a police car, talking into the radio microphone. "What happened?" Nancy asked him.

He put the microphone down and said, "The Kiley house has just been robbed!"

10

Skating Secrets

Nancy, George, and Bess followed Officer Brody to the Kileys' front yard. Neighbors and children were gathered behind a yellow tape that read Do Not Cross.

Nancy put a finger to her lips and pointed to the backyard. Bess and George followed her over to the chain-link fence. Nancy found the hole and squeezed through, followed by George and Bess.

They searched the ground first for clues. Nancy knelt next to a basement window and saw dog tracks. She followed them along the flower bed, leaned down for a closer look, then saw a pair of paws.

Nancy looked up. She was face-to-face with Buster, who was growling. "Whoa." Nancy stood up. "Good dog . . . um . . . I thought you liked me, Buster. Remember?" Buster stopped growling. He studied Nancy for a moment, then turned and walked away.

"Buster is trampling the evidence!" George whispered.

Bess was frozen. "H-h-how did he—" she stammered.

Nancy knelt down again and examined the ground. "Buster provided one answer, anyway," Nancy said. "Judging from the size of his feet, these dog tracks can only be his."

"And the tracks at the Larsen house were just as big," George said.

"If those were Buster's tracks at the burgled houses," Nancy said, "then Mrs. Mendenhall may be our culprit. Buster might be following her when she goes out to break into houses."

The back door opened. One of the triplets— Jamie, Nancy thought—ran out into the yard. "My plastic fire truck is gone!" Jamie cried out. "It was in the sandbox. Someone took it!"

Nancy knelt down and put her arm around him. A burglary had to be especially hard on a child. "What color was it?" she asked. "Red?"

"How did you know?" Jamie asked.

"I'm a detective," Nancy said. "Don't worry. I'll find your fire truck."

He ran back into the house. George came up to Nancy, looking thoughtful. "Wasn't Buster chewing a fire truck?" she asked Nancy.

Nancy nodded. "And Juanita said it wasn't hers when I showed it to her."

Nancy looked up at the window above the back porch. It looked as if the frame had been jimmied. This burglary fit the pattern.

Mrs. Kiley came out of the house. "Ms. Drew," she said, "I'm glad to see you on the case. Juanita told me you were a detective."

"Hello, Mrs. Kiley," Nancy said. "These are my friends, Bess Marvin and George Fayne. I'm sorry this happened. When was the house broken into?"

"Some time last night, according to the police. We returned from the family reunion at two o'clock this afternoon," she said, and shook her head sadly. "Our security alarm didn't go off."

Jamie ran out of the house again, followed by Robbie and Corey. "Our magic lady coins are missing!" Robbie cried, running up to his mother.

"The police won't believe us!" Corey added.

Mrs. Kiley patted Robbie's blond curls. "You probably just misplaced them," she said.

Jamie walked over to Nancy and held out his hand. "I still have mine," he said.

Nancy took the coin and held it up to the sunlight. It looked like the coin Carlos had been playing with—it said Magic Coin on it. She couldn't see a lady on it anywhere. "Was this one of the coins Diego gave you guys after the magic show?" she asked.

"How did you know?" Jamie asked. "You're a great detective." Nancy smiled as she gave the coin back to him. "Don't worry, guys," Jamie said to his brothers. "She'll find your coins. She's looking for my fire truck, too."

Mrs. Kiley thanked Nancy, George, and Bess and held open the gate to let them out of the yard. As they walked back to the Mustang, Nancy said, "The Kiley house was robbed soon after the birthday party." She looked at Bess and George. "Could someone at the party be involved?"

"Carlos was sure he saw someone in the basement," Bess said.

"And the way he acted—I'm sure he was telling the truth," Nancy said.

"So who was at the party? George asked. "David was there, and he's a former Secure employee. In spite of what he's said, he could know the security codes. And he has a crowbar. Juanita could be helping him by giving him information about the families."

Bess frowned. "Not Juanita," she said firmly, leaning against the Mustang. "Mr. Gardner and Mrs. Mendenhall are acting more suspicious, don't you think? Mr. Gardner was at the birthday party, too, and he was lurking in the neighbor's bushes."

"Mrs. Mendenhall wasn't at the party, but she has wire cutters," Nancy said. "Buster has been wandering around in yards where he shouldn't be, and he had a fire truck that might be Jamie's." Nancy opened the car door. "Maybe those VCRs and other things in Mrs. Mendenhall's trunk were the stolen goods. I think we'd better go talk to her."

Mrs. Mendenhall was in the front yard when the Mustang pulled up to the curb. Nancy parked behind a van that said Animal Control. Mrs. Mendenhall was shaking her finger at a woman who was holding a clipboard.

"It wasn't my dog you saw—Buster is in his yard. See?" Mrs. Mendenhall said, pointing to Buster, who was in the backyard, sprawled in front of his doghouse, chewing on a bone.

The woman flipped the papers on the clipboard. "We have a dozen reports that a Doberman pinscher has been running all over town," she said. "Your neighbors have said they've seen your dog jump the fence. This is a violation of the leash law. It's also not safe for your dog or for children. If I catch him where he doesn't belong, I'll issue you a citation." The animal control officer got in the van and drove off.

Mrs. Mendenhall glared at Nancy. "What do *you* want?" she demanded.

"Some answers," Nancy said firmly. "We just found out that Buster's paw prints are at the burgled houses in River Estates. Did you know he had a stash of plastic toys in his doghouse?"

"My Buster? Plastic?" Her jaw dropped.

Nancy nodded. "And you have a pair of heavy-duty wire cutters, which you could have used to cut a hole in the Kileys' fence. You also had a trunkful of TVs and VCRs the other day. Frankly, Mrs. Mendenhall, you're beginning to look like the River Estates burglar."

"Me? A burglar?" she gasped. "I was storing that stuff for a friend who's moving. If you don't believe me, I'll give you his phone number!"

Nancy pulled out her notebook. "I'll be glad to check it out." Mrs. Mendenhall recited the number, and Nancy wrote it down. She looked at Mrs. Mendenhall. "What about the fact that Buster's tracks are all over the yards of the burgled houses?" she asked.

"Buster *has* been jumping over the fence," Mrs. Mendenhall admitted, "but I didn't know he was stealing plastic toys. I've tried to walk him more. In fact, that's why I had to cut that fence."

"The Kileys' fence?" Bess asked.

Mrs. Mendenhall frowned. "I was walking Buster Saturday morning when he pulled away from me and tried to jump into the Kileys' yard. He caught his paws in the chain-link," she explained. "The Kileys weren't home, so I found some wire cutters in their shed and cut a hole to get him loose."

"But why didn't you tell the Kileys?" George asked.

"Because I was afraid," Mrs. Mendenhall said. "Those rich folks are always looking for a chance to sue somebody."

"You may not be the burglar," Nancy said,

"but you've been spreading rumors that Juanita and her boyfriend are thieves. Why are you doing that?"

Mrs. Mendenhall threw up her hands. "I don't know whether they're burglars or not—I just wanted people to think Juanita couldn't be trusted so she couldn't extend her play group to every day. I have to get my sleep. I can't stand the noise!"

"Well," Nancy said, "I'll let you work out the details with Mr. and Mrs. Kiley about paying for fixing the fence, but I expect you to stop bad-mouthing Juanita. Agreed?"

"Agreed," Mrs. Mendenhall said.

Nancy, George, and Bess got back in the car and drove toward Nancy's house. "So can Mrs. Mendenhall be eliminated as a suspect?" Bess asked from the backseat.

"Probably," Nancy said. "But I think we should make some phone calls and check out her story." Nancy grinned and shook her head. "I don't know how Mrs. Mendenhall is going to keep Buster from stealing toys."

George laughed. "At least we know it wasn't the burglars who were stealing toys—it was Buster."

At Nancy's house, George called Mrs. Mendenhall's friend, who confirmed what she had said about the items in the trunk. And Mrs. Mendenhall's boss told George that Mrs. Mendenhall had been at work on the nights of the burglaries.

Nancy glanced at her watch. It was 3:30—almost time to help Juanita at the skating rink. But something was bothering her about the Kiley burglary.

"It's just a hunch," Nancy began, "but if the Kileys were robbed right after a birthday party, then maybe the birthday party itself is important. What if there were birthday parties at the other burgled houses—before the burglaries?"

"If the same person was at all the parties, he could case out each house," Bess said.

Nancy nodded. "David would be at all the parties if Diego was putting on a magic show." Nancy got up. "I'll call the Mowrers, Larsens, and Bairds." She picked up the phone and called each family.

When she was done, she stared at Bess and George. "Can you believe it?" she asked.

"Incredible," said George.

"Amazing," said Bess.

Nancy held up her hand and counted on her fingers. "One: The Mowrers had a birthday party on March fifteenth, and their house was robbed on March eighteenth. Two: The Larsens had a party on March twenty-second, and their house was robbed on March twenty-sixth. And three: The Kiley party was on Saturday, and they were robbed last night or this morning."

George sat up straighter. "Wow—it looks like there is a birthday party connection," she said. "But what about four, the Bairds?"

Nancy checked her notebook. "The house was robbed on March twentieth. But they haven't had a birthday party. Hmmm."

Bess looked at her watch, then jumped up from her chair. "You'll have to figure it out later, Nancy. Juanita's waiting for us at the skating rink."

Rock music echoed off the walls at the rink as skaters whirled around the floor.

Nancy picked out a pair of skates and pulled them on, then stashed her shoes in a locker. She rolled up the sleeves of her white blouse and smoothed her blue skirt. She spotted Juanita, who was trying to keep Carlos, Michael, and Sara skating clockwise around the rink. Nancy went onto the floor and joined them.

Bess had Mitchell, Kyle, and Brian, who were hanging onto her flared pink skirt. In bicycle shorts and a roomy T-shirt, George took charge of Michael and Carlos, racing them past most of the crowd while Sara stayed with Juanita.

Nancy swayed to the beat and started skating, enjoying the rhythm and the exercise. "You look great tonight, Nancy," Max said as he skated up to her and matched her pace.

"Thanks," Nancy replied. "What are you doing here? I thought you had a million jobs that kept you busy."

"Skating's great exercise. It helps me unwind

after a hard day," Max said. "But what I enjoy most is the magic business. Look, I've been practicing," he continued. He dug into his pocket and pulled out a quarter. He tried to palm it the way Diego did, but he fumbled and dropped the quarter. It went spinning away and landed next to the barrier.

Nancy tried not to laugh. "I guess you need a bit more practice," she said. Max went off to retrieve the quarter, and Nancy searched the crowd for Juanita but saw Ian MacDonald instead. He was talking to David near the edge of the rink. This was the last place she expected to see Mr. MacDonald. He was waving his hands as if he were describing something to David.

"That's Ian MacDonald with David. Do you know him?" Max asked when he returned to Nancy's side. Nancy nodded, and he added, "Ian is probably trying to sell David a new magic prop." Max grabbed Nancy's hand. "Come on, Nancy, let's show these slowpokes how to skate."

Startled, Nancy followed Max gamely as he raced with her around the rink. Finally, he skidded to a stop and looked at his watch. "Sorry," he said, "but I'm late for one of my jobs. See you later, okay?"

"Sure," Nancy answered. Breathless, she looked for Ian MacDonald again, but he was gone. David was now talking to Juanita. George and Bess still had all the children in tow, including Sara. Then Nancy saw Max stop beside David and tell him something. David nodded, then Max waved and left the rink.

Skating around the rink with Max had left her hot and thirsty. Nancy decided to get a drink at the snack bar before she joined George and Bess to take her turn at baby-sitting. Sipping a lemonade slowly, she stretched her break to ten minutes. Bess came skating toward her. Nancy tossed her cup into the trash. "I'm coming!" she cried, and skated to meet Bess.

"George lost Carlos!" Bess clutched Nancy's shoulders. "You've got to help us look for him."

"Carlos could get into trouble with *ten* baby-sitters watching him," Nancy said. "I'm sure he's around here somewhere." Looking for Carlos among the skaters, she skated around the rink twice. She went back to the snack bar and looked under the tables. Then she saw the rear exit.

Nancy opened the door into an alley and heard a muffled cry. She listened, trying not to breathe.

She heard banging. It was coming from a Dumpster next to the building. Then she heard a child sobbing. Nancy half-skated, half-ran to the Dumpster and threw open the lid. Carlos was inside. He looked up at her, tears streaking his face.

"Oh, Carlos," Nancy said. "How did you— never mind. Can you grab my hand?" She leaned down, reaching for him, but wasn't close enough. She leaned in farther until she was on tiptoe, balancing on the edge of the Dumpster, stretching as far as she could. "Carlos—take my hand!"

Carlos's fingers touched Nancy's hand. Then she froze in horror. Someone had grabbed her legs and flipped her body up and over the edge of the Dumpster.

Nancy fell hard into the bottom of the Dumpster. The lid slammed down, leaving her in the dark, facedown in garbage.

11

The Baby-sitter Is Missing

Nancy landed on a bag of garbage that smelled like onions and cigarette ashes. She coughed and tried to sit up.

"Ow! You're squashing me!" Carlos yelled.

"Oh—sorry," Nancy said. She moved forward on her knees in the darkness, her hands out to feel for the Dumpster wall. "Sit still, Carlos. I'll try to find something to get us out." She groped among the garbage bags, holding her breath as sickening smells surrounded her.

Finally, Nancy found what felt like a broken broom handle. She reached up and pushed the handle against the Dumpster lid. In the welcome burst of light, Nancy could see Carlos huddling at the bottom of the Dumpster, holding his nose.

Nancy propped up the Dumpster lid with the broom handle and lifted Carlos up and out of the Dumpster. Then she climbed out herself, brushing her hands through her hair and hoping she didn't have any garbage stuck in it.

Carlos wrinkled his nose as Nancy knelt down next to him. "Boy, do you stink!" he said.

"I think we *both* do, Carlos," she said, frowning. "Now, how did you get in the Dumpster?"

Carlos's brown eyes were solemn. "It was a masked man! He grabbed me and took my gold!"

"Gold?" Nancy asked. "What gold?"

"My magic gold coin!" Carlos cried.

Magic coins again? Nancy thought. The Kiley children had said they were missing their magic coins, too.

Nancy looked down at Carlos. "Do you mean the coin Juanita let you keep from your grandfather's bag?" she asked.

Carlos nodded, then shuddered. "That bad guy grabbed me and put me in the trash! Call the police!"

Nancy put her arm around him. "We'll do that. Let's go, Carlos." She opened the door to the rink and guided Carlos back inside.

The music was rocking with a faster, harder beat, and the rink was full of dancing teenagers. Adults searched for shoes and helped children out of their skates. Nancy saw Bess and George trying to find out which shoes belonged to which of the five of the play group children, who were gleefully sliding on the floor in their socks.

Nancy and Carlos went up to Bess and George and told them what had happened in the alley.

"How awful," Bess said. "Are you all right?" she asked Carlos. He nodded and looked at the skaters as if he were searching for someone.

"I'm going to call the police," George said, and headed for a phone booth.

Bess brushed a carrot peel from Nancy's shoulder, then ran off, crying, "Carlos, come back here!"

Nancy scanned the crowd. Where was Juanita? That's odd, Nancy thought, as she looked around the rink for the third time. Juanita didn't seem to be in the rink at all. And David was gone, too. It was hard to believe Juanita would leave the children for any reason.

Nancy pulled her skates off and put on her shoes. Then she looked through the locker area and the snack bar for Juanita. She had disappeared. Nancy walked back to stand beside George against the lockers. Bess was telling a story to five fascinated children as they sat on the carpet. Carlos was putting on his shoes.

"I hate to say this," Nancy whispered to George, "but Juanita *did* ask us for help tonight—she made sure we'd be available to take over for her. If she and David were planning to skip town, this would be the perfect opportunity."

George nodded. "If David is missing, too, then Officer Brody will think they left town with the stolen goods," she said.

Carlos jumped up. "Nita's not a burglar! Some-

96

one kidnapped her!" He swung his leg back and kicked Nancy's shin—hard.

"Ow!" Nancy bent over and grabbed her leg.

"Carlos! You know it's not nice to kick people," George told him.

Nancy rubbed her leg and looked at Carlos. His forehead was creased with worry lines. She sighed. Naughty or not, Carlos must be frightened for his sister.

"We'll find Juanita, Carlos—I promise," Nancy said. "I was just thinking out loud. Juanita isn't a burglar." Carlos's face brightened. Nancy hoped she was telling the truth.

When the police arrived, Nancy whispered to George and Bess, "Don't tell the police Juanita's missing. They won't consider her a missing person until she's been gone forty-eight hours, so they won't investigate, anyway," Nancy explained. But if Juanita is the thief, Nancy thought, then keeping silent could mean she was getting away.

Nancy stayed next to Carlos while Officer Volpi, a petite, blond police officer, questioned him. But the story had grown in Carlos's mind. "It was a masked man," he said, "and he had giant hands and a big nose." Officer Volpi looked doubtful but said she'd look into the matter.

When the parents of the play group children arrived, Bess and George covered for Juanita. "She's not available right now. Can I give her a message from you?" Bess asked cheerfully.

George smiled and said they were Juanita's new assistants. When all the play group children had gone, Nancy, George, and Bess left the rink and took Carlos home.

At the Puentes house, Juanita's grandfather stroked his chin as Nancy told him Juanita was missing. "I'm sure she's all right if she's with David," he said uncertainly. "You don't think that anything . . . happened to her, do you?"

Nancy gave him a sympathetic look. "I hope she'll show up soon," she said. It was hard to reassure Diego when she herself had so many questions about Juanita's disappearance. She waved goodbye to Carlos and left to join Bess and George in the Mustang.

George leaned over the front seat as Nancy pulled out of Diego's driveway. "Where to, Nancy? Can you think of any place we should look for Juanita and David?" she asked.

"Let's go to the Magic Shop—maybe David and Juanita went to his apartment."

Nancy drove slowly down Front Street past the Magic Shop. It was closed and dark. There was no light on in the apartment above the store, and David's truck wasn't there.

"I think I'll drive to Hancock tomorrow and visit Ian MacDonald," Nancy said. "He was talking to David at the skating rink. Maybe David told him something about his plans." Nancy turned around in the driveway.

"Why don't you telephone him?" George asked.

"I want to see his place," Nancy said. "Can you guys check back here tomorrow morning to see if David comes back?"

"No problem," George said.

The next morning Nancy called Diego and learned that Juanita still had not come home. This made her even more determined to go to Hancock, which was about twenty miles from River Heights. It was a small town—only five shops were open on Main Street when Nancy got there. She followed a winding road and parked in front of a brick building with an old canopy over the door. The sign on it read MacDonald's Magic Supplies.

She walked through the front door into the display room. Magic props were displayed on shelves and boxes were stacked against the walls.

Mr. MacDonald came out of the back. His red-brown eyebrows formed into peaks. "Hello, Ms. Drew. What a surprise. Don't tell me you're in the market for magic."

Nancy smiled. "Not unless you know how to make people disappear. Juanita didn't come home last night, and we don't know where David is. I saw you talking to him at the skating rink last night. Max said you were probably telling him about a new magic prop," she said.

Ian MacDonald nodded. "Diego wasn't home when I called," he said, "so Juanita told me I could talk to David at the rink."

"Did David say anything to you about leaving town or mention any plans he had with Juanita?" Nancy said.

Mr. MacDonald looked thoughtful. "Let's see. I asked him to tell Diego about the prop. . . ." His eyes lit up. "You know, he *did* mention something about needing a vacation. And he said he was leaving very soon."

"It's odd that he didn't mention it to Diego," Nancy said.

The bell rang over the door. A tall, bald man walked in and looked around. Mr. MacDonald hurried over to talk to him. "Your order came in, Mr. Denisen. It's in the back room." The two men went into the back.

Nancy wandered around the shop. On a shelf near the back room was a set of linked metal rings. Nancy picked it up and idly tried to separate the rings. They came apart, fell with a loud clatter, and rolled all over the room.

Nancy scrambled to gather up the rings. One had landed near the door to the back room. As Nancy bent to pick up the ring, she heard Mr. Denisen ask, "Do you have them yet?"

"I'm working on it," Mr. MacDonald replied.

"How did you ever find them? Was there an inside guy at the Mint?"

"I can't talk right now. I'll let you know," Mr. MacDonald said.

Nancy picked up the ring, wondering about what she had overheard, and wandered to the front of the store. "An inside guy at the Mint": What did Mr. Denisen mean? The door to the back room opened, and Mr. MacDonald ushered Mr. Denisen out the front entrance.

He came over to Nancy and said, "Oh—I see you found the new prop. The rings have a special ratchet to make them extremely easy to separate." His blue eyes twinkled.

Nancy grinned. "You're right about that. I just chased five rings around the room," she said.

Mr. MacDonald laughed. "Well, come back sometime, and I'll see if we can find another toy for you to play with. Oh, by the way, have you seen Max since last night?"

"No," Nancy said. "Did you need him for something?"

Mr. MacDonald looked tense for a moment, then said, "Not really. But he borrowed something from me and hasn't returned it yet."

"Well, if I see him, I'll let him know you're looking for him," Nancy said.

She drove back to River Heights, thinking about what she'd seen and heard in Hancock. When she reached River Heights, she decided to head for the Puentes house first to see whether Juanita had returned.

When Nancy rang the doorbell, Diego opened the door instantly, a hopeful expression on his face. But when he saw Nancy, his face fell. "Come in," he said sadly.

"Hasn't she even called?" Nancy asked.

Diego ran his hands through his hair, making it stand up in tufts. "I haven't heard a word. It's not like her—making her old grandfather worry so much."

Nancy felt a lump forming in her throat as she thought of how Diego would feel if his granddaughter turned out to be a thief.

"Could I look in Juanita's room?" she asked. "Maybe there's a clue up there."

Diego nodded and pointed upstairs. "Be my guest. Maybe you can say a cheerful word to Carlos. He's very worried about his sister."

Nancy climbed the stairs and found Carlos in his room. He was sitting on the bed, playing absently with some coins. He stacked them up, then knocked them down, then sighed and started to stack them again. Diego must have given up hiding the coins from him, Nancy thought.

"Hi, Carlos," she said. "Can I see your treasure?" She bent down to look at the coins.

Most of the coins were the same ones she had seen before, with the words *Magic Coin*. But some of them pictured a woman dressed in a flowing gown. Nancy picked one up and studied it. Someone had mentioned coins with a lady on them. But who?

"Give that back," Carlos said. He snatched the coin out of her hand. Then he scooped up the others, put them into the bag, and tucked the bag in a drawer.

"How would you like to help me find Juanita?" Nancy asked. "I'm going to her room to investigate. Can you tell me where it is?"

"I'll show you," he said cheerfully, and led Nancy to Juanita's room. It didn't look as if Juanita had planned to go anywhere. Her drawers and closet were full of clothes, and her psychology textbook was open on the desk.

Carlos picked up a pencil from the desk and pulled out some papers from his pocket. "I'm going to take notes, too," he said. A scrap of paper fell on the floor.

Nancy bent down and picked it up. It was a piece of letterhead stationery. Under the heading Secure Monitoring Company was a River Estates address—Reese Gardner's. And beneath the address were the words *Master Code*, followed by a series of numbers.

What was Carlos doing with Reese Gardner's security code?

12

Chasing the Codes

"Where did you get this?" Nancy asked, holding out the paper.

Carlos looked scared, then cried out, "It's mine!" He snatched the paper from Nancy's hand and ran into the hallway and down the stairs.

"Carlos—wait!" Nancy yelled. The front door slammed. She raced down the stairs two at a time. Carlos was jumping onto his bicycle when Nancy opened the front door.

He sped away down the sidewalk. Nancy ran after him, but Carlos took shortcuts through his neighbor's backyards. Nancy shouted quick apologies to people as she dashed into and out of their yards.

Nancy heard a hoarse barking. Buster jumped over the fence and caught up with Carlos, who stopped and gave him a pat. Nancy ran faster, hoping Buster would distract Carlos long enough for her to catch up. She hadn't known Buster and Carlos were such good friends.

Buster barked, then ran away from Carlos toward Nancy. She stopped, gasping for breath. The last thing she needed was another challenge from Buster. But wagging his tail, he ran up to her and licked her hand. "Good dog," she said, patting his head.

Carlos had taken off again and was riding on the sidewalk. Nancy and Buster chased him. Out of the corner of her eye, Nancy saw a car driving slowly down the street behind her.

When she slowed down, the car slowed, too. Nancy turned her head. It was Reese Gardner, and he was definitely following her.

Annoyed, Nancy ran up to the window of the car. Mr. Gardner jerked his head back, startled. Buster ran past Nancy and jumped in front of the car.

Mr. Gardner slammed on the brakes. The car stopped short of hitting Buster. Before Nancy could open her mouth, Mr. Gardner shot out of the car and began to run. Buster ran after him and jumped on his back, knocking him into a hedge.

"Help!" Mr. Gardner yelled. He tried to scramble out of the hedge, but Buster's powerful jaws were clamped on his leg.

Nancy stood over Mr. Gardner. "I'll help you," she said, "but I want some answers first."

Mr. Gardner grunted and tried to open Buster's jaws. Buster held on stubbornly, shaking his head from side to side as if he were playing a game. "What answers?" Mr. Gardner asked. He settled back into the hedge.

Nancy tapped her foot on the sidewalk. "First—why were you following me?" she asked.

Mr. Gardner sighed. "I was hoping you'd lead me to David," he said. "I'm sure David is the burglar. That's why I've been following him and searching his truck. The police have questioned me three times. If someone doesn't find evidence against David soon, they'll try to pin the burglaries on me and I'll lose my visitation privileges with Jimmy. The police know that I knew the Larsen code and that I'm a convicted felon."

Nancy gave him a doubtful look. "All this sneaking around and spying was to try to solve the mystery yourself?" she asked.

"Something like that," Mr. Gardner admitted. "Look, if you call off this stupid Doberman, I won't interfere again. But you've got to find the burglar."

"Nancy!" It was Bess. She and George pulled up to the curb in George's car. "What happened?" she cried. "We were following Mr. Gardner's car, but he lost us."

George grinned and said, "I'd say Buster has the case wrapped up."

"Not quite," Nancy said. "I don't think Mr.

Gardner is the burglar. Here, Buster, here, boy—come here!"

Buster let go of Mr. Gardner's leg and jumped to Nancy's side, playfully grabbing her arm. "Easy, boy," she said, carefully withdrawing her arm from between his teeth. "Yuck," she said, and wiped her arm on her jeans.

Nancy held out her hand to Mr. Gardner, but he ignored it and awkwardly rolled onto the sidewalk and stood up. He dusted himself off and walked over to his car.

Nancy told Bess and George what Mr. Gardner had said. "So I guess we can eliminate him as a suspect," she said.

George watched Mr. Gardner get in his car, then turned to Nancy. "If he's no longer a suspect, and Mrs. Mendenhall is eliminated— because she was just storing those things for a friend—then the only suspects left are David and Juanita," she said.

"Not Juanita!" Bess exclaimed. "It must be David—right, Nancy?"

Nancy frowned. "David seems the obvious choice because of his connection to Secure," she said. "He has a crowbar and a rope ladder. Don't forget, too, that Juanita knew the Larsens' code. The fact that they disappeared together makes them both look guilty."

She looked up and down the sidewalk. "Carlos!" she said. "Where did he disappear to? He ran away with an interesting piece of evidence. He's got Mr. Gardner's security code."

"How did Carlos get Mr. Gardner's security code?" George asked.

"I don't know," Nancy admitted. "That's why I was chasing him, to see if he'd tell me."

Bess patted her shoulder. "I'm sure you'll crack this case soon," she said firmly. "Do you want a ride back to Juanita's?"

"Thanks, Bess," she said. "But no thanks on the ride. I'll walk Buster back to Mrs. Mendenhall's. I'll meet you guys over there. And see if you can find Carlos. He's on his bike."

Nancy whistled to Buster, who surprised her again by trotting up to her side. She walked down the sidewalk toward the Puentes house. Nancy looked into each yard she passed, but she didn't see Carlos anywhere. Other children in their yards smiled and shouted, "Hi, Buster!" as she and the Doberman walked by.

"Looks like you've been running around making friends, Buster. Better not tell your mistress. She thinks you're a vicious guard dog."

A man who was trimming his hedge stared at her. "Now I'm talking to dogs," she said, sighing.

"It could be worse. You could be talking to an unemployed magician." The voice startled Nancy, and she jumped. Max Karn had appeared beside her.

"Where did you come from?"

"My car ran out of gas," he said. "I was on my way to see Diego. He said on the phone that with David gone, he may not open the store for a while and was going to cancel the magic show at the next birthday party. I'm afraid I might be unemployed if I can't persuade him to change his mind."

Nancy gave him a sympathetic look. "Good luck. By the way, did you see David and Juanita leave the skating rink last night?" she asked him.

Max shook his head. "I left before David."

Buster gave a bark, ran down the sidewalk, and jumped over the fence around his yard. Max whistled through his teeth and said, "That Doberman is really something. I bet he can get into any yard he wants to."

Nancy laughed. "And he's been in a lot of them, believe me," she said. "Oh—I almost forgot. Ian MacDonald is looking for you."

Max pulled his collar away from his neck. "Oh yeah? Did he say what he wanted?"

"He wants you to return something, I think," Nancy replied, wondering why Max had grown so tense.

As they walked up the front steps of the Puentes house, Max said, "I'll drive out to see him soon." He rang the doorbell.

Diego answered the door, looking pale and shaken. He held out a piece of paper to Nancy. She took it from Diego's trembling fingers. Letters that looked as if they'd been cut from a magazine were pasted on the paper.

She read the words: DELIVER BAG OF MAGIC GOLD COINS TO DOCK #5 BY MIDNIGHT. JUANITA DIES IF YOU CALL POLICE."

13

Kidnapped!

Nancy's hands began to shake as she read the paper again. Juanita had been kidnapped! Carlos had been right.

Max leaned over her shoulder, took the paper gently from her hands, and read it. He handed it back to Diego, and said solemnly, "Diego, I'm so sorry. Please let me know if there's anything I can do." He patted Nancy's shoulder. "I'll see you later, Nancy," he said.

Nancy looked at Diego's pale face, then took his arm. "Let's go in and sit down," she suggested. She led him to the living room where Bess and George were already sitting.

"Carlos came home on his own," George told Nancy.

"Glad to hear it," Nancy said. She turned to Diego. "Can you think of any reason why

111

Juanita's kidnapper would want those coins?" she asked.

Diego shook his head. "They're just base metal coins with no value," he said.

Nancy sat on the edge of her chair. "These are the coins you give out at the birthday parties, right?" she asked. Diego nodded, and Nancy went on. "I've spoken with the families whose houses had been robbed. Three of the four families had birthday parties with your magic show as the entertainment a few days before the burglaries. Do you remember how many coins you gave away at the Mowrers', the Larsens', and the Kileys'?"

Diego pulled on his mustache. "Yes, that's easy to remember," he said, "since I let only the birthday child keep a coin. I gave away one to Melissa Larsen, one to Stephanie Mowrer, and one each to the Kiley triplets. Oh, and one to Amy Baird. Six in all."

"Wait," George said. "The Bairds didn't have a birthday party."

"That's right," Diego said. "But Stephanie Mowrer and Amy Baird have the same birthday, so they had a party for both of them at the Mowrer house. Oh—and I gave one to Jimmy Gardner at the party his father gave for him. That makes seven."

Nancy stood up. "Each of the burgled families mentioned that some of the kids' things were missing—" Nancy began.

"Right!" Bess exclaimed. "Mrs. Mowrer told me her daughter had a coin stolen from her room."

"I have a hunch," Nancy said, "that the birthday parties and the coins Diego gave away could be the clues to solving this case."

Diego looked bewildered. "But they're just worthless coins! Why would someone rob a house or kidnap Juanita for them?"

"That's what we need to find out," Nancy said.

Diego stood up. "I'll go get the bag."

"I'll go with you," Nancy said. "I need to talk to Carlos."

Diego nodded, and Nancy, George, and Bess followed him up the stairs. Carlos was in his bedroom. He hung his head and stuck out his bottom lip when he saw them.

"Carlos," Nancy said, "I need to see that paper in your pocket, and I want you to tell me exactly where you found it—okay? It might help me find Juanita."

Carlos scuffed his foot against the floor. "Me and Jimmy got it from his father's basement," he said. "It was on the wire things—taped and taped all around." Carlos dug his hand into his pocket and handed Nancy the paper.

"That looks like the paper I was trying to get at the Gordon house. Remember? It was wrapped around the security wires," George said.

Nancy nodded, staring at the paper. Bess and George looked over her shoulder.

"Wow," George said. "It's got the security code and Mr. Gardner's address."

"If Carlos got this from the Gardners' security wires," Bess said, "and you saw a paper on Mr. Gordon's wires, and they both have Secure systems—then is the paper supposed to be there?"

"I tried to find out, but I couldn't," Nancy said. "But if a burglar knew the paper was there, he could get the code just as Carlos did—and come back and break into the house! Maybe Carlos *did* see a man in the Kileys' basement. Someone at the birthday party could have sneaked down into the basement and taken the paper."

Diego looked confused. "But I've already spoken to Carlos about this man he saw. It was probably Max," he said. "He usually hides the dove cages in the basement before the magic act. Then he retrieves them while the kids are distracted by the rainbow and the coin tricks."

Nancy scratched her head. She remembered seeing Max in the Kileys' kitchen, putting doves in his pockets. Did Max take the paper? Was he the burglar? No time to think about this now, she thought. We need to find out more about the papers. "I'm going to call Secure Monitoring Company again," Nancy said.

Downstairs, Nancy called Secure Monitoring Company. This time, she asked for the district manager. She explained who she was, and the manager listened to her with respect when she said, "I have reason to believe that a paper listing a security code was left on the wires of one of your systems and was then used by a burglar to break into the house. Do your installers leave these papers with every system you install?"

The manager explained, "The papers are supposed to be hidden high on the wires. Only a maintenance person should be aware of them. They contain information that would aid in repairing the system, and yes, they list the security codes. Are you sure the burglar used our paper?"

"It looks that way," Nancy said. "One more question. Why was David Andrews fired from your company a few months ago?"

"Well, Mr. Andrews was late to many of his installation appointments. He was spending too much time working at another job, at a magic shop, I believe," the manager said, then he sighed. "Unfortunately, the man we hired to replace him had to be fired, too, after botching some installations. His name was Max Karn."

"Max Karn—young, dark hair, tall—that Max Karn?" she asked.

"Yes, that sounds like him," he said.

"Thank you, you've been very helpful," Nancy said, and hung up the receiver. She turned to Diego. "Mr. Puentes? Could I have Max's address please—he just became a suspect."

Diego's eyes widened, then he left the room to find Max's address. Nancy told Bess and George what the Secure manager had said on the phone.

"We need to check out Max's apartment," Nancy went on. "He could be hiding stolen goods." Diego came back into the room and handed Nancy Max's address. "He lives on Lake Drive," Diego said.

"Let me get this straight," Bess said. "David and Max are suspects because they both knew that Secure Monitoring Company put papers on the wires with the codes. But how do the coins fit into all this?"

"Like this," she said. "We have a kidnapper who's demanded a bag of fake gold coins as ransom for Juanita. Diego gave out some of these coins during his magic shows at birthday parties. The houses where the birthday parties were held were burgled soon after the magic shows by someone who knew the security codes. So someone at the parties knew about the papers on the wires. He or she took the papers from the basements, and later came back and broke into the houses—without setting off the alarms."

George jumped in. "Nancy, that's it! If each of the burgled families are missing the coins Diego gave their kids *and* missing the papers on the wires in their basements, then the houses were robbed to get the coins back! The burglar took some TVs and things, but whoever it was was

116

most interested in the coins, because valuable things were usually left behind."

"Let's confirm this with phone calls," Nancy said. She called the Larsens first. Mrs. Larsen confirmed that Melissa had complained that her coin was missing. The story was the same at the Mowrers' and the Bairds'—each child's coin was missing. They were all puzzled by her request to check the wires in their basements, but all had the same answer—no papers.

"So, the Mowrers, the Bairds, and the Larsens are all missing coins and the Secure papers," Nancy reported. "There was no paper on the wires in the Kileys' basement, so it must have been removed during the magic show—before I went down to investigate. And Robbie and Corey Kiley told me their coins were missing when I talked to Mrs. Kiley after the burglary."

"But one of the Kiley kids still has his coin, Nancy—remember?" Bess pointed out.

Nancy bit her lip, thinking. "That's right," she said. "It said magic coin on it. But Robbie and Corey said their lady coins were missing." She turned to Diego. "Some of the coins Carlos had today were different from the others. Do you remember giving out any coins with ladies on them?"

Diego shook his head. "I just grab a handful of coins and put them in my pocket for the coin tricks," he said. "The ones I bought from Ian

117

MacDonald said Magic Coin. Here—I have the bag." He picked up the bag from a low shelf.

Nancy dumped the coins onto the table. She sifted through them and found five that had a woman in a long gown. The rest of the coins said magic coin on them. She studied one of the coins with the woman, then looked up in wonder. "This coin says U.S. twenty dollars, and has a date—1933."

The others gathered around the table and looked at the coins. Nancy took a piece of paper and a pencil from her purse. She put the paper over the coin, then rubbed the side of the pencil over the paper. "There," she said, "now I've got a rubbing of the coin."

Nancy scooped the coins into the bag and handed it to Diego. "Keep these safe until we can arrange the ransom drop," she said. "We'll go to Mr. Baird's now and show him this rubbing. He's a coin collector—he'll know if the coin has any value. The kidnapper might want the bag of coins because of the coins with the woman."

Diego gave Nancy a worried look. "Will this help you find Juanita?" he asked.

"If we find the thief, we'll also find the kidnapper," Nancy said softly. "Let me check out a few things, then I'll call Officer Brody and we can arrange the ransom drop-off."

"The note said not to call the police," he said.

"We need the police, Diego. Otherwise, the kidnapper could pick up the ransom and never return Juanita," Nancy said gently. "Officer Brody is good at his job—he'll make sure his people are well-hidden at the ransom pickup site."

Diego nodded, but the lines across his forehead deepened. He got up and took some sandwiches in plastic wrap from the refrigerator. "You girls should eat lunch—take these with you," he said. He handed the sandwiches to Bess. "I'll wait here with Carlos. Maybe Juanita will call, or David. Maybe it's all a mistake or a bad joke."

Nancy stood up. "We'll see you soon," Nancy said, knowing in her heart that most ransom notes were not mistakes.

Mr. Baird led Nancy and her friends into his study. Nancy showed him the rubbing of the coin, and he peered closely at it. "This looks like a twenty-dollar Saint-Gaudens Double Eagle gold coin! The woman pictured is Lady Liberty. Remember I told you I was getting ready to buy one of these before my coin collection was stolen. But the coin I wanted was a 1911 Saint-Gaudens Double Eagle. If I'm reading the date correctly—1933—then *this* Double-Eagle coin is illegal!" he told Nancy.

He slapped the rubbing onto the desk and picked up a book. He flipped the pages and pointed to a photograph of a coin. "This is it," he said. "Over 445,000 twenty-dollar Saint-

Gaudens Double Eagle gold coins were minted in 1933. But that year President Roosevelt was trying to lift the nation out of the Great Depression, so he made it illegal to own gold coins. The 1933 coins were never released to the public. All the gold coins stored in the Treasury and bank vaults were rounded up and melted down."

Nancy studied the photograph. "Melted down? Then how could Diego have one?"

"Or five?" asked Bess.

Mr. Baird tossed the book on the desk. "Coin collectors have often speculated that an employee at the U.S. Mint might have taken some of the Double Eagles before the meltdown began," Mr. Baird said.

As soon as he said, "Mint," Nancy remembered the conversation she'd overheard between Ian MacDonald and his customer, Mr. Denisen. Could Mr. MacDonald know something about these particular coins? Diego had bought the bag of magic coins from him.

"Nancy," Mr. Baird said, "if you know the whereabouts of any of these illegal coins, you should contact a U.S. Treasury agent."

Nancy smiled. "I think you might have had one of the illegal coins in your house," she said. "The coin your daughter complained was stolen could have been a Double Eagle."

Mr. Baird stared at Nancy. "What!" he exclaimed. "Amy had a 1933 Saint-Gaudens Double Eagle—in my house? I can't believe it!"

"If my hunch is right," Nancy said, "it may have been why your house was burgled. And I think I know who might be involved. May I use your phone?"

Mr. Baird pointed to the one on the desk. Nancy called Officer Brody and told him that Juanita had been kidnapped and why the kidnapper asked for the bag of coins as ransom. Then she asked him for the name and number of a Treasury agent in Chicago.

"I've been in touch with an agent named Edward Simmons," Officer Brody said. He gave her Simmons's number and said the River Heights Police Department would do their utmost to get Juanita back safely.

Nancy called Mr. Simmons, who confirmed that the 1933 coin was illegal. "It would be priceless to an unethical collector," he said.

"Can you meet with me in River Heights?" Nancy asked. "I need your help."

"Agent O'Hare and I can meet you in a couple of hours," Mr. Simmons said. "We've been tracking a suspect in the River Heights area. We think his business is a front for selling stolen rare coins. Maybe you know him. His name is Ian MacDonald."

14

A Golden Lady

Nancy's mind raced. She remembered the day Ian MacDonald had come to the Magic Shop. He'd told Diego he'd confused two of his orders and wanted to see the bag of coins he'd sold him. The pieces of the puzzle clicked into place one by one. Mr. MacDonald must have put the Double Eagles into the bag with the magic coins for safekeeping—and then accidentally sold them to Diego.

That was it! Diego told Ian MacDonald he'd already given away some of the coins at birthday parties, and he couldn't find the bag, though he thought Carlos might have had it. Mr. MacDonald could have tried to get his rare Double Eagles back by breaking into the houses, and when he only found a few, he tried to get the rest from Diego directly. And when that didn't work—he kidnapped Juanita!

"I've met Mr. MacDonald," Nancy told the Treasury agent on the phone, "and I think you're right about the stolen rare coins." She told him what she'd reasoned out.

"We'll try to make the ransom drop-off a trap for the kidnapper. Are you sure it's Mr. MacDonald?" the agent said.

"No," Nancy said thoughtfully. "I've got to think about this some more."

"We'll be in River Heights by eight tonight. Why don't you meet us at the police station?"

Nancy agreed to meet them and hung up the receiver.

Mr. Baird looked at her in admiration. "That's quite a story," he said.

"Wow!" George exclaimed. "Rare coins, Treasury agents—real gold! Incredible."

"Please don't tell anyone about the kidnapping, Mr. Baird," Nancy said. "It would put Juanita in great danger."

"Of course not. Good luck."

"Thank you for your help," Nancy said. "Everything makes sense now—almost. There's one more person I have to speak to, so we'd better be on our way."

Once they were in the car, Nancy headed for Lake Drive.

"Where are we going?" asked Bess.

"I have some questions to ask Max," Nancy answered. "We need to think this all out very carefully," she added. "At Diego's house, I counted five Double Eagles mixed in with the bag of magic coins."

"I remember," said Bess.

"Diego gave away some of the Double Eagle coins, not realizing what they were."

"And you said Ian MacDonald was breaking into houses to steal them back," George said.

"Don't forget we have some sandwiches here," Bess said.

"Later, Bess," George said. "But how would Mr. MacDonald know who Diego gave the coins to?"

Nancy drummed her fingers on the steering wheel, thinking. "That's where Max comes in!" she said. "I saw Max examining the triplets' coins after the Kiley magic show, so he must have been checking to see if Diego gave them any of the Double Eagles."

"So you think Max is working for Ian MacDonald?" George asked.

"It would make sense," Nancy said. "Mr. MacDonald probably knew that Max had an inside knowledge of security systems, which is why Mr. MacDonald recommended Max to Diego as an assistant."

Nancy made a left turn on Lake Drive, looking for Max's address. "Remember," she added, "Diego said that before each birthday party Max hid the dove cages in basements. Down there, he'd pick up the security paper. After the magic show was over, he'd check the kids' coins to see whether any of them were the gold ones. If so, he'd break into the house using the security code."

"One thing doesn't fit, though," George said. "No party was held at the Baird house. How did Max get that code?"

"I don't know," Nancy said. "He must have gotten the paper somehow, because the house was robbed five days after Amy Baird and Stephanie Mowrer had their party at the Mowrers' house."

"There's another thing that doesn't fit," Bess said. "When Diego told us which kids were given birthday coins, he mentioned Jimmy Gardner. But the Gardner house wasn't robbed."

"Carlos had the paper with the Gardner security code, remember?" Nancy said. "He'd probably been playing in the basement with Jimmy and had removed the paper with the codes," Nancy said, shaking her head. "How did he get that paper? He must be part monkey."

Bess laughed. "You don't know the half of it," she said.

"So Max couldn't rob the Gardner house because he didn't have the code," George said. "Pass me a sandwich, Bess."

"Wait," Nancy said. "We're almost there."

At the end of Lake Drive, Nancy parked in front of an old two-story brick building. "I don't see Max's car in the parking lot. Maybe we can find a way to get into his apartment and look around for evidence," she said.

Nancy, George, and Bess climbed the outside stairs and tried the door. It was locked with a dead bolt and wouldn't budge. They went back downstairs and around to the back of the building. "Look—the window's open," George whispered to Nancy.

"Good. And that tree next to it should get us high enough to climb in," Nancy said.

"This isn't exactly legal," Bess insisted. "What if someone catches us?"

Nancy sighed. "I know it's not legal, but Max or Mr. MacDonald climbed into enough upstairs windows to rob those houses. Maybe climbing into this one will help us put them in jail," she said.

"Oh—all right. Someone boost me up," Bess whispered. Nancy boosted Bess up to a low branch, where she waited while George and Nancy climbed past her. Nancy saw Bess look around. "This is risky, Nancy—in broad daylight," Bess said nervously.

"We'll just have to be careful," Nancy whispered back. She leaned into the window, crawled over the sill, and helped George and Bess. They spread out to search the apartment.

A green-and-white striped sofa was against one wall, with a desk facing it across the room. A hallway led to a tiny kitchen and bathroom.

Max's answering machine and telephone

were on the desk. Nancy rewound the tape and played it.

"Mr. Karn?" a voice said. "This is Patrick Cochran. The coin you inquired about—an early '30s Double Eagle—can be worth several thousand dollars, depending on the condition. Bring it in and I'll take a look at it. My number is 555-8439." Nancy turned off the tape.

"Max is trying to find out how much the Double Eagle is worth. But if he's working with Ian MacDonald—wouldn't he know this?" Nancy asked.

"Maybe Mr. MacDonald is taking advantage of Max, using him for the burglaries but not telling him the value of the coins," George said.

"Could be. Let's hear more of the tape." Nancy turned the machine on again. After some beeps, a hoarse voice said, "You know who this is, Karn. Call me about the merchandise."

Nancy narrowed her eyes. "Let's search the apartment. Maybe we can find the merchandise."

In the hall closet, Nancy saw boxes full of old athletic equipment, shoes, and old clothes. She and George searched through every box, but none hid TVs, VCRs, or coins.

Bess, who had crawled under the desk, cried, "I think I found something. This drawer is too shallow—it has a false bottom in it!"

She stood up as Nancy and George rushed over to the desk. Bess pulled out the center drawer. She felt around the edge of the drawer until she found a catch at the back. She pressed it and the bottom of the drawer flipped open, revealing a compartment.

Nancy reached in and pulled out three cardboard tickets. They were receipts from pawn shops in different parts of the state.

"This one's for a TV and VCR," she said, "this one's for another VCR, and the last one is for a TV." She pulled her notebook out and wrote down the names of the pawn shops and receipt numbers.

"Whew!" George said. "It looks as if Max has been pawning stolen goods! Maybe that second message on the answering machine was a fence asking for more merchandise."

"But that means Max must have more stolen goods somewhere," Nancy said, "if he only pawned some of them. Where's the computer? Let me check that closet again."

She stood up in the closet and studied the ceiling. "There's a trapdoor," she said. "Give me a boost."

George boosted her up, and Nancy pushed on the door. It gave way, and she stuck her head above the ceiling. "It's an attic storeroom," she said. She scrambled through the opening. "Yes!" Nancy cried, her voice muffled by the attic. "More VCRs, CD players, two portable TVs, and one laptop computer. I'll find the serial numbers."

Nancy wrote down the serial numbers of the

items in the attic. "We have our evidence—let's get out of here and call the police," she said.

George helped her down. The three of them scrambled out the window and climbed down the tree.

Nancy called Officer Brody from a phone booth near a supermarket and told him what she'd found.

"Of course we didn't break in," she said, crossing her fingers. "Would I do a thing like that? Let me give you the serial numbers so you can check whether they match any of the stolen goods. I have some pawn shop names, too."

Nancy recited the numbers and names.

When she finished, Officer Brody said, "The Treasury agents told me about MacDonald's involvement in all this. I'll see you at the station house later tonight."

"Okay," Nancy said, and hung up the receiver. She hurried back to the car, where George and Bess were finally eating the sandwiches.

"Pot roast," Bess said. "And here's a soda. I ran into the supermarket and got them."

Nancy took the sandwich and soda and began to eat, thinking hard. She wanted to go back to Mr. MacDonald's shop in Hancock. Juanita could be hidden there.

Nancy swallowed the last sip of soda, and headed the Mustang for Hancock. When they pulled into the parking lot, Mr. MacDonald's shop was closed, the curtains drawn shut.

The front door was locked by two dead bolts, but George found a small side door that led to a loading ramp. Nancy took her lock-picking kit from her purse. It took her a few minutes, but she finally got the door open. The girls climbed up the ramp and into the shop.

"It's empty! You should have seen all the stuff that was in here this morning," Nancy said, her voice echoing in the room.

"I'll look upstairs." George went up to the second floor while Bess and Nancy checked out the back room. It was empty too, except for a tall wooden cabinet with double doors.

Nancy opened the doors and heard a muffled groaning. She looked around the cabinet, but it was empty. She heard another groan, louder than the first.

"What *is* that?" Bess asked.

"I don't know," Nancy said, "But this looks like a trick cabinet. There must be a hidden compartment."

Nancy stepped into the cabinet, her hands shaking a little. The groaning sounded as if someone was hurt. It could be Juanita.

Nancy pressed both hands along the back of the cabinet and finally felt something smooth and cold. She stepped back, letting more light into the cabinet, and stared at her reflection.

Two mirrors met in the middle of the cabinet, angled toward her. When she'd first looked in the cabinet, the mirrors had reflected the wooden sides, which made it seem she was looking at the back. Nancy found a groove, fit her fingers into it, and tugged. The mirrors slid to the sides of the cabinet.

A weight fell into her arms. She staggered back, then looked down. It was David.

15

Deadly Waters

Bess rushed to help Nancy lay David on the floor. His face was bruised, and Nancy touched his neck, feeling for a pulse.

"Is he breathing?" Bess asked anxiously.

George came into the room and said, "The upstairs is—" She stopped, her breath caught in her throat. "David! Is he all right?" she asked.

Nancy frowned. "He's breathing, but he looks as if he's been beaten pretty badly. Better call an ambulance, Bess." Bess ran into the front of the shop.

"There's a blanket in the trunk. George— could you get it?" Nancy asked, and handed George her car keys.

When George returned with the blanket, Bess was with her. "The ambulance is on the way," she said. "Can we do anything to help him, Nancy?"

Nancy spread the blanket over David. "Just keep him warm," she said, "in case of shock." She looked up at her friends. "If MacDonald could do this to David, what does he have planned for Juanita?"

"We have to find her somehow, Nancy," Bess said.

David stirred slightly, moving his head and mumbling, "Juanita . . . lady . . . luck . . ."

George knelt by his head. "Shh, David . . . it's okay," she said softly. She looked up at Nancy. "He must be delirious."

The Hancock paramedics arrived and they loaded David carefully into the ambulance.

The girls watched the ambulance drive into the night from the parking lot. "This case is getting dangerous, Nancy," Bess said, her hands shaking.

"Mr. MacDonald is dangerous, and Max probably is, too," Nancy said quietly. "But maybe we can outsmart them and find Juanita before anyone can harm her. Let's move it!"

They dashed to the Mustang and headed back to River Heights. They had an appointment at the police station with the Treasury agents.

Officer Brody led them to a meeting room when they arrived a short while later. Two men stood up when they entered, and Officer Brody made the introductions. Edward Simmons was a short, heavyset man with dark hair. Walter

O'Hare was taller than Simmons, with red hair and green eyes.

They sat down at the table, where a map of the dock area was spread out. Agent O'Hare began to detail the ransom drop-off.

"Ed and I will be on a boat on the opposite shore from dock number five," he said, pointing to the map. "As soon as the kidnapper picks up the money, we can pursue him—if he escapes by boat."

"I'll be with three officers," Officer Brody said. "We'll hide in the warehouses. We want you next to the Magic Shop in the first alley opposite dock number five, Nancy. Make sure Diego comes back to that same alley after he places the coins on dock five."

"Where do you want me?" George asked.

Mr. Simmons pointed to a place on the map a short distance from the dock. "You can watch for boats approaching from that direction. Ms. Marvin will be in a parked car near the second alley and can alert Ms. Drew if anyone approaches on foot or by car from Front Street."

Bess seemed relieved that she'd be in a locked car, and Nancy threw Officer Brody a grateful look. He winked at her, and Nancy smiled.

The meeting over, Nancy drove Bess and George home to change into dark clothes.

Three hours later Nancy looked up at a glowing full moon. She was hiding behind two trash cans in the alley opposite dock five. The moon would make it harder to stay hidden, but it would also make it easier to see Ian MacDonald when he picked up the coins.

Nancy leaned forward to watch Diego, who was waiting in the alley in front of the trash cans, clutching a bag of coins. He cleared his throat. He's nervous, Nancy thought. Not that I blame him. I'm nervous, too.

It was close to midnight, and the dock area was deserted. The river made soft slapping noises against the dock, and a police siren wailed somewhere in the distance.

Nancy heard Diego clear his throat again. He walked slowly past her to dock five. The tower clock at City Hall struck twelve deep bongs as he reached the end of the dock. He set down the bag of coins and hurried back to the alley, looking nervously over his shoulder.

Nancy motioned him behind a Dumpster, then she hurried and crouched behind the trash cans again. Carlos was just above her, asleep in David's apartment on the second floor of the Magic Shop, supervised by a baby-sitter.

Nothing happened for several minutes. Nancy waited tensely in her hiding place. Her eyes were beginning to hurt as she stared, barely blinking, at the bag of coins. MacDonald was probably checking the dock area for police. He was too smart not to expect a trap—she just hoped they could outsmart him.

135

Nancy heard a splash. She turned toward the river and saw a hand come up over the edge of the dock. It grabbed the bag of coins and disappeared. Someone was in the water under the dock.

Nancy crept forward and heard another splash after the hand disappeared. MacDonald must have swum under the dock, Nancy thought. The water had to be ice cold this time of year. He must have on a wet suit. She wondered whether the agents had seen him from their boat.

Nancy stayed in the shadows for a moment. Officer Brody and the undercover officers dashed out of a warehouse and headed for the shoreline. Nancy ran toward the dock and saw George running to the shore, followed by Officer Volpi. The police were running along the water's edge, looking for the kidnapper.

Alone on dock five, Nancy searched the area desperately, looking behind the barrels and crates stacked near the dock. Would MacDonald have stashed Juanita somewhere nearby while he picked up the coins?

Nancy heard a car door slam, then more running feet. "Nancy—where are you?" Bess yelled from the second alley. "Diego's hurt!"

Bess must have seen Diego from the car. But what was Diego doing in the second alley?

Nancy rushed toward Bess's voice, then gasped. A man leaped out from behind a barrel.

He clamped his hand over her mouth and pulled her off her feet. She squirmed to get free and saw his face—it was Ian MacDonald!

"Nancy!" Bess called again. She sounded farther away.

Mr. MacDonald dragged Nancy backward along the docks. Finally, he stopped and pulled her behind a stack of crates on dock three. He took his hand away from her mouth but kept a tight grip on both her arms.

Nancy gasped for breath. "You have the coins now, so let Juanita go!" she cried.

MacDonald glared into her eyes. "Shut up! That double-crossing idiot Max stole the coins before I could get here."

Nancy's breath caught in her throat. The Treasury agents, the police, and George were all following Max! No one was left to help her, except Bess, and Nancy couldn't hear her any longer.

She thought about kicking MacDonald hard in the shins, but then wondered if she shouldn't let him take her hostage. If she went where he wanted to go, he might lead her to Juanita.

MacDonald pulled a length of rope out of his pocket and jerked Nancy's hands behind her back. "I thought Max was stealing the Double Eagles for *you*," Nancy said, hoping to stall him. He began to twist the rope around her hands.

"He double-crossed me!" MacDonald said in a

fierce whisper. "He kept one of the Kiley kids' coins and the one he got from Carlos when he knocked him into that Dumpster."

Nancy fought to stay calm and remembered the rope trick David had showed her. She clutched a small loop of rope in her fist before MacDonald knotted the rope around her wrists. "But weren't you there when he took Carlos's coin?" she asked.

"No! I'd already left the rink. I'd lured Juanita and David outside the rink and locked them in the trunk of my car," MacDonald said. "I was too busy to watch Max. I thought I'd get back at him by not letting him in on the ransom pick-up. But he found out somehow, hid under the dock, and took the coins!"

Nancy remembered how Max had peered over her shoulder at the ransom note at Diego's house.

"No more questions!" MacDonald growled. He moved in front of her and pulled another piece of rope out of his coat pocket. He knelt to tie Nancy's feet. He wasn't going to take her with him, she realized. She kicked out, knocking him backward, and ran. Enraged, he scrambled to his feet and tackled her. With her hands tied, Nancy fell hard on the wooden dock, her left shoulder burning with pain.

MacDonald tied her feet together. Then he grabbed her by the shoulders and dragged her over to a crate. He picked her up and threw her inside it. Nancy screamed for help as she fell into the coffinlike crate. Maybe Bess would hear her, wherever she was.

"No coins, no Juanita," MacDonald said, grinning down at her. "And now—no Nancy Drew!"

MacDonald slammed a lid on top of the crate, and Nancy lost sight of the moon and stars. She struggled frantically inside the crate, trying to get free of the rope around her wrists. Then she heard a pounding. MacDonald was nailing down the lid!

Nancy screamed again. She felt the crate tip over and over on the dock and couldn't stay on her feet. The crate stopped moving for a second, then it toppled over the edge of the dock into the river.

16

Carlos to the Rescue!

The jolt of impact with the water sent shock waves through Nancy's body. She took a deep breath as the icy water swished through the slats of the crate. It floated for a second, then sank.

Nancy fought down panic. The water felt like a block of icy steel on her chest, weighing her down. She held her breath, her heart beating rapidly.

Nancy touched the small loop of rope in her hand. She had just enough slack to loosen the ropes on her wrists. Nancy worked both of her hands free. She twisted around to untie her feet. But the knots were too tight, and her lungs, desperate for air, were ready to burst.

Nancy pushed with her head at the top of the crate, then turned and kicked it hard with her feet. Nothing happened. She kicked again. The top of the crate splintered.

She tore out enough slats to pull herself through, and swam up, propelling herself toward the surface.

Nancy drew in a deep lungful of air, her chest aching as she coughed. It was impossible to tread water with her feet still tied, so Nancy swam forward, pulling hard with her arms.

When she reached the dock, Nancy hung onto the edge, shivering. In a few minutes her breathing had become normal again. Using all her strength, she hoisted herself out of the water and rolled onto the dock. She lay still for a moment, then sat up and worked on the wet ropes around her ankles.

When her feet were finally free, Nancy stood up, her clothes dripping. She jogged in place to keep warm and scanned the dock area but didn't see anyone. Where was Bess's car? And the police? Her eyes fell on a cabin cruiser tied up at the dock. The name on the side was easy to see in the moonlight: *Cruisin' Carla.*

In a flash, Nancy remembered what David had said as he lay wounded in Ian's shop. He'd mentioned Juanita's name and then said "lady luck." Maybe that was the name of a boat. Was Juanita hidden on a boat?

Nancy trotted along the dock, looking at the names of the boats. At least three were moored at each dock. Some were small pleasure craft, others were fishing boats. But they all looked dark and deserted.

Then she saw a dim light. Nancy ran toward it and saw a small cabin cruiser rocking gently at dock ten. The cabin window was dimly lit, as if from a flashlight. She looked for the name on the side. It was the *Lady Luck!*

Nancy leaned over and grabbed the rail on the boat. She pulled it closer and climbed over the rail.

She tiptoed across the deck to the cabin door, opened it carefully, and climbed down the ladder to the cabin. A portable lamp stood on a table, which was flanked by bunks on both sides under the portholes.

A blanket covered something on the nearest bunk. Hardly daring to breathe, Nancy crept forward, hoping it wasn't Ian MacDonald, lying in wait, ready to spring out at her.

She clutched the edge of the blanket and pulled it off the bunk. Juanita was lying there, her hands and feet bound with rope. Duct tape covered her mouth, and her eyes were wide open.

"Oh, Juanita," Nancy cried, "are you hurt?" She pulled the tape off Juanita's mouth, and Juanita screamed. It was a scream of warning, not pain. Someone slammed his fists into Nancy's shoulders and knocked her to the floor.

Nancy twisted around, ready to fight. Ian MacDonald was grinning down at her. Striking out with her fists and feet, she fought him with all her strength. He grunted when Nancy's heel connected with his stomach, but he grabbed her foot and tried to flip her.

Nancy hooked his ankle with her other foot and he tripped and fell hard on the empty bunk.

"Carlos to the rescue!"

A black furry body flashed past her, and she heard a deep growl. Buster crashed into Mac-Donald, knocking him to the floor. He tried to crawl away under the table, but Buster jumped on his back, pinning him flat.

Carlos slid across the cabin floor in his socks and fell on top of Buster. MacDonald groaned. Nancy stood up and helped Carlos to his feet, but Buster stayed with MacDonald, low growls coming from his throat.

"Come back here, Carlos." It was Bess's voice—she was outside! But it was George who clattered down the ladder into the cabin first. Bess, the police, and the Treasury agents were right behind her, filling up the small cabin.

George flipped on the overhead light. She grinned at Nancy, then hurried over to Juanita and untied the ropes. Carlos was on the bunk next to Juanita, hugging her. Buster still had MacDonald pinned, and Officer Volpi was trying to get him off.

Bess pushed through the crowd to Nancy. "Oh Nancy—I'm so glad you're alive!" she said, and hugged her. "After I saw MacDonald drag Diego into the second alley and just leave him, I called

143

you. When you didn't answer, I drove off for help and found a police officer. We came back, picked up Diego, and drove him to the hospital."

"Is Grandfather all right?" Juanita asked. By now she was sitting up, massaging her wrists.

Bess waved her hand. "Oh, he's fine. But he has a bump on his head," she replied. "But, Nancy, when I got back to the docks, George ran past me, chasing Carlos. Then Carlos yelled out that some bad guy had drowned you!"

"He tried," Nancy said, "but a little of David's magic saved my life." She told them how she'd used David's rope trick, then asked, "Where's Max? Did he get away?"

George shook her head. "Agent Simmons and Agent O'Hare got him. But I realized that Mac-Donald was still at large," she said, "so I ran back to the docks. That's when I saw Carlos, and he yelled that you were in trouble."

Nancy turned to look at Carlos, who was hanging onto his sister as if he'd never let her go. "How did you know I was in trouble, Carlos?" Nancy asked.

"That silly baby-sitter Grandpa hired fell asleep," Carlos said. "I was looking out the window to see what was going on. I saw the bad guy put you in a big box and kick it in the water!"

Carlos waved his hands. "So I sneaked downstairs and went outside. I looked all over in the dark. Then Buster came and we saw you climb on that boat. So we came to rescue you!"

"I'm so glad you did," Nancy said. "Is it all right if I give you a hug to thank you?"

"I guess so," he said. Nancy wrapped him in her arms and squeezed. "You're a great detective," she said. Carlos hugged her back, then went over and sat beside his sister.

"Did I save you, too?" he asked.

"You sure did," Juanita said, hugging him. "With a little help from Nancy." She smiled at Nancy.

By now Officer Volpi had removed Buster from Ian MacDonald's chest, and Officer Brody had handcuffed him. The other two officers led him off the boat. Buster went over to Carlos and sat down, panting. Carlos scratched his head.

"Good work, Drew," Officer Brody said to Nancy. "I'll meet you in an hour at the Puentes house. I'll need statements from all of you."

An hour later Diego handed out hot chocolate and doughnuts to his guests. He had a bandage on his head, but he insisted he felt fine and refused to let Juanita get up from the sofa.

"Shouldn't I go see David at the hospital?" she asked her grandfather.

Diego shook his head vigorously. "No—you rest," he said. "David has a concussion and lots of bruises, but he'll be home tomorrow. I told him Nancy found you."

Nancy had a blanket around her shoulders, and was sitting in Diego's favorite armchair. Officer

Brody took another doughnut. "Max didn't get too far with those coins," he said. "Simmons and O'Hare caught up with him and recovered them." He nodded his head at the Treasury agents, who were sipping their hot chocolate.

"Did he confess?" Nancy asked.

Officer Brody nodded. "He admitted to using the magic shows as a way to get into the basements and pull the security papers off the wires. Then he and MacDonald would come back to break into the houses and search for the gold coins Diego had given away."

"But why did MacDonald sell that bag of coins in the first place?" asked George.

"I can answer that," Agent Simmons spoke up. "MacDonald had mixed twelve 1933 Saint-Gaudens Double Eagle gold coins into a bag of magic coins to hide them from people like us."

Nancy nodded. "That's what I thought."

"But he accidentally switched this bag with another bag full of fake coins," Agent O'Hare said, "and sold the one with the Double Eagles to Diego."

"How did MacDonald get the coins to begin with?" asked Bess.

Agent Simmons set down his mug. "The government has long suspected there was a conspiracy at the Mint all those years ago. Illegal Double Eagles keep popping up now and then. Someone could have stolen the coins before the Gold

Order was signed, and then hid them to keep them from being melted down."

Officer Brody swallowed the last of his doughnut. "When MacDonald realized he'd sold the gold coins to Diego, he recommended Max to Diego as a new assistant. Max had stolen coins for MacDonald in the past," Officer Brody said.

"But Diego always kept the keys on his belt, and Max didn't want to arouse Diego's suspicions by breaking into the trunks in the Magic Shop to look for the coins." Officer Brody finished his hot chocolate and put the mug down.

"When Max began to help at the magic shows, he realized Diego was giving away coins to children—and some of them could have been Double Eagles. So far all the birthday parties had been in River Estates, which Max knew had Secure Monitoring systems because he used to work for Secure. So he came up with the plan for getting the security codes from the basements during the magic shows."

"Then Max found out MacDonald had misled him about the value of the coins," Nancy said. She told Officer Brody and the agents what she had learned from MacDonald when he was tying her hands. "That's why Max took the bag of coins at the ransom pick-up."

"I can't believe he was in the water in a wet suit," said Bess. "It's so cold." She shivered.

Nancy started counting in her head, trying to

figure out where each of the valuable coins had ended up. "So Diego gave two Double Eagles to two of the Kiley triplets," she said. "One went to Stephanie Mowrer, one to Amy Baird, and one to Melissa Larsen. And Carlos had one on him at the skating rink, and Max stole it. That adds up to six coins."

"And you said there were five Double Eagles left in the bag," Bess said.

"Then where's the other Double Eagle?" Agent O'Hare asked.

Nancy thought for a moment. "Jimmy Gardner must still have it," she said. "Diego had given it to him during his birthday party. But the Gardner house wasn't robbed because Carlos and Jimmy had removed the paper with the code from the security wires."

Agent O'Hare whipped out a notebook and wrote down Reese Gardner's address.

"One thing puzzles me," Nancy told Officer Brody. "How did Max get the code from the Baird house? There was no birthday party there."

Officer Brody shrugged. "I guess he found a different way to get into the basement."

Juanita sat up. "Oh, I remember now. Max stopped by the Bairds one day when I was babysitting. I think it was the day before they were robbed," she said, wrinkling her brow in concentration. "Yes, it was! He told me his car had broken down and asked to use the phone. He must have sneaked down the basement while I was in the kitchen with the kids."

"So what will happen to the illegal Double Eagles?" George asked.

"Illegal Double Eagles," Carlos said. "Hey, it rhymes, sort of."

"So it does," said Agent Simmons, and he smiled at Carlos. "After we question MacDonald about where he got them, the illegal Double Eagles will be turned over to a museum. They'll eventually go on display."

Dragging a sleepy Buster by the collar, Carlos pushed his way through the crowd of legs to the coffee table in front of the sofa. Carlos cleared his throat and yelled, "Introducing—Carlos the Great!" He picked up the TV remote and clicked on the set, turning the volume to blast. Buster began to bark. Everyone winced and covered their ears, except Diego, who stood up and headed for Carlos.

Carlos calmly clicked the button again on the remote and turned off the TV. "See—it's magic!" he said, and grinned.

George looked at Nancy, and Nancy laughed. "You're a great magician, Carlos," Nancy said. "Does anyone have a treat for Buster?"

American SISTERS

Join different sets of sisters as they embark on the varied, sometimes dangerous, always exciting journeys across America's landscape!

West Along the Wagon Road, 1852

A *Titanic* Journey Across the Sea, 1912

Voyage to a Free Land, 1630

Adventure on the Wilderness Road, 1775

Crossing the Colorado Rockies, 1864

Down the Rio Grande, 1829

Horseback on the Boston Post Road, 1704

Exploring the Chicago World's Fair, 1893

Pacific Odyssey to California, 1905

by Laurie Lawlor

Published by Simon & Schuster